LOVE IS TWO PEOPLE TALKING

A Novel By
CHARLES H. BANOV, M.D.

EveningPostBooks
Our Accent is Southern!
www.EveningPostBooks.com

Published by
Evening Post Books
Charleston, South Carolina
www.EveningPostBooks.com

Copyright © 2012 by Charles H. Banov, M.D.
All rights reserved.
First edition

Editors: John M. Burbage, Holly Holladay
Design: Gill Guerry

No part of this book may be reproduced or transmitted in any form or by any means, electronic or mechanical, including photocopying, recording or by information storage and retrieval system – except by a reviewer who may quote brief passages in a review to be printed in a magazine, newspaper, or on the Web – without permission in writing from the publisher. For information, please contact the publisher.

First printing 2012
Printed in the United States of America

A CIP catalog record for this book has been applied for from the Library of Congress.

ISBN: 978-0-9834457-5-3

Charles H. Bawar, M.D.

ACKNOWLEDGEMENTS

This story is about two of the most intimate human emotions, love and communication within a family. I have received much encouragement and support from my family, my editors and my many colleagues and friends. Editor Stephen Hoffius and publisher John Burbage were always available to me despite their demanding schedules. I appreciate the suggestions of editor Janet Hulstrand. My wife, Nancy, my children Drs. Mark and Michael Banov, and my daughter Lori Banov Kaufmann were strong critics of every phase of the work. Thanks to my sisters, Caren Masem and Linda Stern for their unending enthusiasm throughout the writing of this story.

DEDICATION

This book is dedicated to my youngest daughter Pamela, who has Rett Syndrome, and to the millions of people worldwide who struggle every day with Parkinson's disease. I also dedicate this story to the medical researchers who are working to solve these mysteries.

INTRODUCTION

What would I have thought 40 years ago if I saw the shaky old man I've become, wobbling along, watching every step for fear of toppling over, unable to open the coffee shop door without help, sitting in a corner out of the way, using both hands to lift a cup to his lips, spilling as much as he drank? Would I have done anything differently then if I knew what I know now that I am 80 years old?

I feel like I fell into a vat of starch and just crawled out. I freeze suddenly in mid-stride as if my shoes were covered with glue and stuck to the pavement. It takes me twice as long now to get out of the bed in the morning and dress myself. I'm unsteady on my feet. Sometimes I suddenly lose my balance and fall. I'm forgetful and have difficulty swallowing. My handwriting looks like a doctor's prescription.

I have Parkinson's disease. I'd heard of it when I was a young man but didn't know what it was. I know about Parkinson's now. I live with it every day.

Medical knowledge has changed drastically in my lifetime. For example, Rett syndrome, a disability that plagues my granddaughter, didn't even have a name when I was young. The disorder affects females mostly, and they hardly talk or walk. But some girls scream a lot — loudly and piercingly — for what seems to be no good reason. Rett victims are hyperactive sometimes and need constant care. People like my granddaughter were rarely seen on the streets back then. They usually stayed in institutions where others fed them, dressed them and changed their diapers when necessary for their entire lives.

I own a pawnshop on Main Street. I started working there in high school. The store belonged to my father, who worked there all his life for his father, who immigrated to America from Eastern Europe in the 1880s and opened the business in the middle of town. My grandfather's name was Samuel Geller. He called the shop "Uncle Sam's." He was an observant Jew and very proud to become an American citizen. People enjoyed coming in to see him and his business grew steadily.

Pawnshops aren't as popular as they used to be. But Uncle Sam's is different. Lots of folks still stop in — young and old, men and women. Some wear white collars and others blue, so to speak. They enjoy looking around and they trade and buy things — jewelry and watches especially.

My father, Daniel Geller, and I were close. We worked together until the day he died. He spoke frankly to me the way a father should speak to his son. He gave me good advice. "Don't get deep in debt buying merchandise, and don't price things too high. Customer service is everything," he warned. That's what my grandfather told my father, and that's what my father told me, and we've done well with Uncle Sam's for almost 100 years.

I've never been rich, but I've never been strapped for cash either. I could afford to get married and to buy a house in a nice neighborhood. I owned two cars — neither fancy — one for my wife, Sandy, and one for me. I paid for my son's college and medical school. Jeffrey is a dermatologist now and has his own practice. He's married with two children, both girls. I wanted him to do better than my grandfather, my father and me. But don't get me wrong. I've always had everything I needed — not much more, but certainly no less.

I pretended for the longest time that I had everything together in my life. But I was fooling myself. My son and I don't have the same relationship that I had with my father, and I regret that. But I'm proud of my son and the man he has become.

My wife died seven years ago. Since then, my life has been stripped away like a dead animal by the side of the road withering a little, day after day, until all that remains is a sunken carcass of skin and bones. Sandy had a mild stroke one morning. I got her to the hospital, where she suffered a second stroke far more severe. She never said another word and could no longer take care of herself.

I was forced to move her into a nursing home, but I visited her every day, sometimes twice. I held her hands, looked into her eyes and told her the best I could what was happening in the world. Every now and then she responded ever so slightly. She tried to communicate with me through little gestures that she could manage. Sandy loved hearing about our granddaughters, Peggy and Kate. I know she did because her lips would curl a little into the vague beginnings of a smile. And I kept her up to date about our son Jeffrey and his wife Carol and the rest of our family. I could tell Sandy was very sad when I told her that her brother died because she wrinkled her brow in a certain way.

My dear wife was in that nursing home for almost a year before she died peacefully in her sleep. I miss her.

It wasn't long afterward that my own health began to fail, slowly at first, but steadily. Parkinson's is destroying my motor skills primarily, abilities I once took for granted — like walking with ease, talking without a struggle, and standing tall and steady. This disease has stolen almost everything from me. But it has given me something, too. Something I will share with you.

Let me take you back to the day that it began.

CHAPTER ONE

It was a glorious morning in early autumn without the heavy humidity of summer. The breeze was gentle and the sky clear. I stood on the porch of my house with my son Jeffrey. We were enjoying fresh coffee. We seldom spent time together, so this day was special. Ironically, it was also the day I received my death sentence.

Jeff is a worrier and always has been. He's college educated, so I figure he worries more intelligently than I do. Because he's a dermatologist, people call him constantly about rashes and dark spots and pimples. They wonder if they have skin cancer mostly. So maybe it's not so strange that when I said I'd tripped on the sidewalk a week before, Jeffrey reacted as if I had tumor on my forehead.

"Jeff, I just bruised my knee. It's really no big deal," I said. But Jeff made an appointment with my doctor, who just happens to be my best friend.

"Look, Dad, at your age, it might be something serious. We don't need to take any chances."

"The pavement was uneven, Jeff. That's all," I insisted.

I've known Saul Goldman since childhood, and I didn't want to bother him at work with something so trivial. I would see him soon enough at our weekly gin rummy game. When you're 80 and run a pawnshop, you've got time on your hands. When you're a physician, you don't. But I agreed to go. That's why Jeff was at my house that morning: to take me to my appointment. I could have driven myself, but my son wanted to make sure I actually went.

• • •

We sat quietly inside Saul's examination room, and as I said, we seldom talked father to son. It was as if we didn't know exactly what to say to each other. Thankfully, Saul walked in after a short time.

"Morning, Sam. I hope you've recovered from that drubbing the other night," he said referring to our weekly card game.

I chuckled.

"Yeah, yeah, so you won three bucks off of me, Saul. You just wait 'til this week's game," I vowed.

He did not respond as he read my chart.

Saul ran me through a battery of tests — stand up, sit down, hold out your arms, stick out your tongue. He studied my hands, then used his little light to look into my eyes.

"Walk across the room," he said. "Now walk back." He asked me how well I was sleeping, how often I went to the bathroom and if I was having sex.

I shot a glance at Jeffrey. "Come on, Saul. Sandy died seven years ago. There hasn't been anyone else."

"Sorry, Sam. I have to ask," Saul said. He looked at his notes and shook his head. "I've been afraid of this. You remember how you discarded last week and almost flung the cards off the table?"

"Uh, yeah … but what does that have to do with anything? My fingers were sticky from those cookies. I won that hand."

"You did win that hand, you're right. But I noticed that you did the same thing with the cards the week before. You held them out and couldn't release them. Sam, you have a problem."

I swallowed hard and felt as if I were waiting for the verdict from the jury foreman: *Your honor, we have reached agreement. We find Mr. Geller guilty as charged and may God have mercy on his soul.*

"Geez, Saul, it can't be that bad."

"Sam, what do you know about Parkinson's disease?" My mind went blank and I felt like time had stopped. My brain reeled at first then latched on to what I didn't want to think about at all.

I remembered watching boxer Muhammad Ali trying to light the Olympic torch in Atlanta. He was no longer floating like a butterfly or stinging like a bee. He was shaking like a leaf. I'd seen people with Parkinson's, their expressionless faces, tremors and hesitant way of moving. Pitiful. I couldn't have that disease — all that shaking and quaking like a milkshake maker.

I wondered if I would look like those rickety people I'd seen in airports — the ones searching desperately for a porter to carry their luggage; standing helplessly waiting for their bags to come around the carousel and knowing they can't lift them. I looked at Jeff, who was discussing the diagnosis with Saul intently. I remember thinking that I could have been walking around the park near my house enjoying a fine fall day, but instead, I was in a doctor's office wondering how long I had to live.

Saul explained that medications would help me considerably but that the disease is progressive and I should be prepared for radical changes in my life.

"You'll need a neurologist to manage your condition," he said.

He said a lot of other things, too, most of which I didn't hear or understand. The pressure in the room was unbearable, as if I were lying on the bottom of a swimming pool.

Saul scribbled something on a prescription pad, handed it to Jeff and smiled.

How can he smile? After all the time we've spent together, how can he issue me a death warrant and smile?

Then he was gone.

"You OK, Pop?" Jeff looked at me, concerned.

"Sure," I replied, not looking up, feeling dizzy.

I tried to stand but couldn't. I felt like the morning after a wild night. But I hadn't been anywhere. Jeff helped me up. The lower half of my body was a melting ice cream cone. I had trouble keeping my balance. I managed to get to the front desk, where Jeffrey made another appointment. I was furious as Jeff walked and I wobbled outside to the car.

"Can you believe that S.O.B.? 'You will continue to have symptoms of Parkinson's until you die. You will most certainly die with it rather than from it,'" I blurted out. "What's that horse shit supposed to mean?"

Jeff looked at me sympathetically but said nothing.

"Does he get a kick out of scaring people?" I asked.

"Saul's just trying to help, Pop."

"Yeah, right," I muttered under my breath.

"Pop, I know this is difficult, but we have a lot to think about and consider."

"We? I'm the only one with this disease, son. It isn't going to affect you. It isn't going to change your life."

"Pop, of course it is going to affect me. Frankly, I think you should move in with us."

• • •

Jeff had always wanted to be a doctor. He did well in college and was accepted into his first choice of medical schools. He selected his specialty with no difficulty, and he married his college sweetheart. Carol understood that he would work long hours and she didn't seem to mind handling household duties.

Jeff was no problem growing up. He never caused us any trouble other than missing weekend curfew a couple of times. I guess you could say Sandy and I got lucky with him. I don't know if it was the product of our parenting or just fate, or maybe a little bit of both. Regardless, I always assumed that Jeff's children would be like him, and I hoped good fortune would come as easily to them as it seemed to come to Jeff.

But then Peggy was born with Rett syndrome. It's a condition whose symptoms are similar to severe autism and a cure has yet to be found. Everything seemed normal for the first year and a half of Peggy's life. I'd like to tell you she was a beautiful baby, but honestly, I've never seen a newborn that is. Pointy head? Matted hair? Scrunched-up face? That's not beautiful. That's not even cute.

Anyway, Sandy and I were thrilled to have our first grandchild. She seemed to be developing normally: walked about age one and grabbed hold of everything in sight; spit up occasionally like all infants do. But almost two years went by and she never said anything that made sense. She just babbled. When Carol asked her to turn off the water in the sink, Peggy turned it on even more, and then she laughed. When Jeffrey asked her to stand up, she ignored him, and just stared off into space without moving. When anyone reached for her, or even looked her in the eyes, she screamed like a banshee.

"She's starting her terrible twos a little early," I'd say reassuringly. But my wife knew something was wrong. "She needs to see a doctor," Sandy concluded.

Carol and Jeffrey first thought it was a hearing problem. But things got worse with time. Peggy grabbed things and threw them on the floor — pictures, books, dishes, glasses — it did not matter. She was an exceptionally destructive child. She seldom slept, often sitting stiffly up in her bed all night with eyes wide open. For hours Jeff and Carol would coax her to lie down, to no avail.

Her screams were hideous. There was no telling when she'd start or when she'd end. She squeezed her eyes shut, opened her mouth wide, clenched her fists and shrieked. Was she in pain? Was she scared? No one knew and she offered no clues. Jeff and Carol would take turns holding her and walking around the room, propping her on one shoulder, then on the other, cradling her in their arms. But she could not be comforted.

Jeff would strap her into a car seat and drive her around for hours hoping to lull her to sleep. He and Carol took turns staying up with her all night. Carol rarely managed to leave the house. But I never heard either one of them complain. They clung to the hope that there was something they could do to turn her into a normal little girl; that there was a magic formula to make everything right.

At first their pediatrician said Peggy was normal — physically and psychologically. But he never tried to eat a peaceful dinner at their house; never witnessed the wailing and destruction. By age 2 she would plop down — it didn't matter where — and refuse to move. When she was urged to stand up, especially if she were touched in any way, she screamed.

Eventually Jeff and Carol learned that Peggy had a condition that could explain almost everything; that she would not be able to function normally for the rest of her life; that she would have difficulty breathing and may have seizures; that her circulation would be poor; that her spine would not develop properly and she would have extreme difficulty walking; and that she'd need almost constant help for practically everything. They realized that caring for Peggy was an enormous challenge, and they accepted it. They threw themselves into doing all they could for their daughter.

Not long afterward, Carol was pregnant with their second child, Kate, who is normal in every way.

• • •

After leaving Saul's office, the only thing I could think about was that a little more than a week before, I was fine. I prepared all my meals, drove to work and back again, visited with friends, played cards — and the worst thing that happened was I lost a few bucks. Now suddenly I saw myself as a burden on my son and his wife who already had their hands full taking care of a grown daughter with the needs of a helpless infant.

I hate to admit this but I couldn't help but think that sharing a house with Peggy was the last thing I wanted to do. Why would I want to share a house with her? Why would anyone? It gave me a headache just thinking about it.

When Sandy died, Jeff suggested that I move in with Carol and him for a while, but I didn't want to leave our house, my home. Being alone there was hard. But I adjusted to living alone and savored my independence. I didn't want to give that up, and I was angry. Not that Jeff had suggested it but because I knew that he was right. Maybe not right away, but eventually I wouldn't have a choice.

Jeff said nothing as we drove away from the office. I suppose he was letting me think and take it all in. But finally he spoke up.

"Don't worry, Pop, I know a good neurologist. His name is Martin Robinson. I'll call him and set up an appointment. It's all going to be OK."

But Jeff didn't look like he meant it.

CHAPTER TWO

I didn't move in with Jeff. Not then, anyway. "Pop, you can't continue rattling around in that big house all by yourself," he said. "It's an obstacle course for you. Suppose you fall and break something. Then you really will lose that independence that you're always bragging about."

"Yes," I agreed, "but don't I lose it if I move in with you, too?"

I wasn't a cripple and I didn't want to be a burden. I convinced myself that my son was overreacting.

The morning after my appointment with Saul, I woke up at 6:30 a.m. as usual in my own bedroom in my own house just like I had been doing for the past 50 years. I fixed my own coffee and enjoyed its refreshing aroma while waiting for the English muffin I had placed in my own toaster in my own kitchen. Sunshine streamed through my window.

Soon afterward I took a walk around the park paying careful attention as I lifted my feet clear of the curbs and uneven pavement. I greeted other folks I see almost every day, remembering all their names and even some of their dogs' names. No one looked at me as if I were a cripple. I'm not a cripple, and I kept reminding myself of that all morning.

Back home, I cleaned up the kitchen and then stepped in front of my special mirror. I needed a haircut but other than that I looked not a day over 75. Damn! How did I get so old?

As usual, the mirror — a seven-foot, gilt-framed antique my grandfather acquired soon after he opened the pawnshop — did not lie. Gramps named it Mr. Truthful and my dad continued the tradition. I shortened it to Mr. T. There are plenty of other mirrors around the house but Mr. T is the most accurate. Mr. T doesn't care what I think. Some folks will stretch the truth when I ask them if my colors match or if they see bags under my eyes. But not Mr. T. If he could speak, he would say, "I call it like I see it."

On this particular morning he pointed out that my hair was thinning. But at least I had some. He noticed approvingly that I had been careful to shave around my jaw and clip the hairs in my nose. One of my gin rummy buddies the other night looked as if he had shaved in the dark. All in all, Mr. T said I was doing alright — and he knows.

I am currently engaged in what I call "creative retirement," which is a nice way of saying, "Leave me alone and let me run my pawnshop as I choose." After more than 60 years in the business, I can take off a day or two without feeling guilty. When I'm not there, my longtime employee, Pat Taylor, takes care of things. But on this day I got there ahead of him.

Before I switched on the lights of the shop, shadows stretched everywhere, from the rows of guitars to the cases of jewelry, the piles of carpenters' tools, the bins of CDs and thousands of other items.

I've seen many things come and go — LP records and 8-track tapes, wide ties, bell-bottom jeans, push lawnmowers, typewriters and 35 millimeter cameras. And most of it sells. People who come to me appreciate things that others have discarded. My clientele includes bankers and bums, old and young, rich and poor, black and white.

The mayor stops by every four years when he's running for office. "How you doing, Pop?" he asks.

I've been around so long almost everyone in town calls me "Pop," especially those who went to school with Jeff. The columnist for the newspaper visits once in a while looking for stories. Some of the customers rib me, saying, "I thought you'd be dead by now" and "It's so sad that you have to work at your age." As if there's someplace else I'd rather be.

I'm an important part of the local economy. Some people have just discovered recycling, but I grew up with it, working with Dad and Gramps. That's what the pawnshop business is all about. One of my many fond memories is helping torment Dad's cousin Alex, who had a pawn shop down the block. They were close friends and fierce competitors.

On a slow day, Alex would think up some excuse to call us, hoping to hear that we weren't selling anything either. He didn't mind if his business was slow as long as things were the same at our shop. So to aggravate his curious cousin, Dad gave me a signal to open the massive brass vintage cash register drawer repeatedly. Alex could easily hear the loud ring on the other side of the phone and he was left to imagine all the business we were doing.

I'm proud of this place; it's one of the oldest businesses in town. In fact, pawn brokering is the other oldest businesses in the world. But pawn brokering is legal.

I took the broom out, swept the sidewalk and nodded to people as they passed. Several stopped and gave me an update on their lives. Elvira, the policewoman on this beat, told me about a theft last night four doors down. A young guy named Augustus asked me for the hundredth time if I'd gotten in a certain rap tape. The banker on the corner said he couldn't wait for the weekend to ride his thousand-dollar racing bicycle, which he purchased from me. The bookstore clerk told me he sent his science fiction manuscript off to yet another publisher.

"How's Jeff doing?" asked Joann Calhoun as she passed by, her weekly apple pie wrapped up in a plastic bag from the bakery two blocks down.

"He's good, thanks," I said. "How about Anna?" Her daughter had taken a break from medical school to work in a clinic in Africa for a year.

"I guess she's fine. Wish she'd write more," she said.

The people who work on our block talk with each other. We share information — good news and bad. We know things about one another. We pick up on the little things that matter because we care. Even though the area has changed a lot since I started working here, people still communicate. And talking isn't the only way to do it, but it sure helps when you speak the same language. Back in Gramps' day, people spoke Polish and German as well as English. It runs the gamut today — French, Italian, Russian, Swahili. Gramps never would have thought people who spoke Vietnamese would live and work in this town.

Just the other day I walked past a café and heard customers seated at the outside tables speaking at least three different languages. They chattered and laughed among themselves. At the Tower of Babel, when people could no longer understand each other, they broke off into separate tribes. It's not like that around here. We figure out how to communicate with one another.

When Jeff was young, Sandy and I would gather up our week-old bread into a plastic bag and drive to the beach. We looked for birds — seagulls, skimmers, even pigeons — but rarely saw any when we first arrived. Then we would throw breadcrumbs in the air and before long a single bird would show up, and another and another. Soon flocks swooped all around us, taking the bread from our fingers before we could throw it. Where did all those birds come from? How did they know we were there? Did they talk to each other with squawks and whistles? Or was it a subtler form of communication that people don't understand?

Bread at the Eighth Avenue pier; that pawnbroker, his wife and kid. Seagull over and out.

Most people are like that, too. When things happen, the word spreads quickly, and that's the way it should be. Which reminds me of my oldest granddaughter. When someone says hello to Peggy, she does not respond. It's like she has some kind of electromagnetic field around her, a shield. When somebody gets too close physically, her shrieks go off like a burglar alarm.

Peggy and her mother have adapted to one another. Carol moves around Peggy like a moon circling a planet. Peggy sits there, looking around. Carol fills a glass with water, places it before her. Peggy drinks, holding the glass carefully with both hands, and then sets it down. Carol gives her another one. Their hands never meet. Carol talks. Peggy listens.

• • •

When Jeff was young I waited for him to ask me questions — about sex, about God, about how to fix a carburetor — but he never did. And since he didn't ask, I didn't offer. I didn't want to impose. Besides, what would I say to him? What do you talk to teenagers about?

It was as if my only son didn't need me. Then he married and began his medical practice, had children of his own and it seemed he needed me even less. I knew more about some of my customers than I did about my own son.

My parents, my brother and I were extremely close. Our religious practices had a lot to do with it. We always spent Saturdays together at home. Saturday is the Jewish Sabbath, which we call Shabbat. It's our day of rest. But times have changed. Now, Saturday is my favorite day of the week to work.

My father would strongly disapprove. As a teenager I argued often with him about how inconvenient it was to stay home on Saturday. It was embarrassing, too. No sports, no movies, no driving, no work of any kind, no nothing on Saturdays. I had to try and explain this to my non-Jewish friends, but few of them understood exactly why. I didn't either back then.

Our family made elaborate plans for the Sabbath. Meals were prepared the night before because it was against the rules to cook on Saturdays. We couldn't drive anywhere, not even to synagogue, which was a mile away from our house. We walked instead. No radio, no television. Come to think of it, television had not even been invented yet. I remember my father asking our non-Jewish neighbors to come over and adjust the thermostat in our house one Saturday. Sabbath rules were that strict.

We were devoted to our religious beliefs and adhered strictly to the restrictions and commandments about Shabbat. On Shabbat, my father, who typically worked 10-hour days, was relaxed and happy. After a leisurely dinner, we sat around our living room and talked about all the things that no one had time to talk about during the week.

When Sandy and I married we tried to follow the old ways but gave up when Jeffrey started school. We were modern Americans and Shabbat traditions were ancient. Looking back on it now, we lost something important when we gave that up.

• • •

I turned the sign in the shop window around from "Closed" to "Open" and headed for my seat behind the counter. The coffee pot hadn't been cleaned the night before, so I dropped the grounds into the trash and started a fresh batch. I thought about calling the deli down the street for lunch in a few hours. They make the best chopped-liver sandwich in town, and they deliver. Well, they deliver to me. It was good to be back in my place. It was good to have a place to be.

My employee, Pat Taylor, walked in the door about a quarter to nine with a worried look.

"Am I late?" he asked, pouring himself a cup of coffee.

"Nope, I got in a little early today. No big deal."

"So what did the doctor say?" he asked.

"He said I'm fine, that I was so healthy I was wasting his time."

Pat didn't look at me as he gathered up his papers from the day before and placed them into separate piles: telephone calls to return, items to be ordered, merchandise to be priced. My father taught Pat the business and we have worked side by side for 40 years.

"Parkinson's, eh?" he said.

I turned away and picked up the glass cleaner and paper towels. "Jeff can't keep his mouth shut," I muttered.

The cases of jewelry have to be wiped down every day to remove fingerprints and dust. We stock 10 cases with necklaces and rings, bracelets, earrings, barrettes, wristwatches and pocket watches. That's where most of our profits are, so I keep the cases looking good, never cluttered, never dirty.

A man walked in the door and headed straight for the power tools. He wore jeans and a T-shirt that said, "I Been Pickin' and Grinnin' at Buzzard's Roost" on the back. His hair was pulled back in a ponytail and he knew what he wanted. Pat waited a few minutes, then walked over and asked if he could help. By the time I'd finished with the cases, Pat had rung up a power saw and extra blades and was giving the man his change. As soon as the customer walked out the door, Pat looked up at me and said, "You knew, didn't you, Sam?"

"Knew what?" I said and grabbed the feather duster again.

"Come on, Sam. Everyone else knew — you stoop over now more than ever."

I glanced down at my feet then pulled back my shoulders as best I could. "I don't stoop over."

Pat rolled his eyes and looked away. "You know, you're just like your old man. I didn't think anyone could be as stubborn as he was, but I was wrong."

"What do you mean by that?"

"He did the same thing. He wouldn't admit that he needed help in his old age and stayed in denial about it until he died. You even look like him now."

"He was not in denial, and neither am I, Pat! I just wish people would mind their own business!"

"Of course he was in denial. And even though he didn't have Parkinson's, he stooped over worse than you. By the time he died he was a foot shorter than he was when I started working here."

"Well, he was an old man! He had a rough life."

"He was 82 when he died. What are you, 80?" Pat asked.

I grimaced. "I'm 80 but I look younger. Everybody tells me so."

"Just like your dad. Spittin' image," Pat said.

There was a display of mirrors across the shop, but I didn't want to give Pat the pleasure of seeing me look.

Why hadn't Mr. T told me this before I left the house?

"Everyone's a doctor these days," I snapped back at Pat. "When did you graduate from med school?"

"I looked it up," Pat said. "You've shown signs of Parkinson's for years. You used to go to the pool to swim a couple times a week. Why don't you do that anymore?"

"Because I'm 80 years old, Pat!" I was losing my patience with this conversation.

"Nope, it's because your muscles don't work right," he said. "And why'd you trip the other day?"

"Like I told Jeffrey, the pavement was uneven. You would have tripped, too!"

"You stumbled last week here at the shop," Pat said.

"When?"

"Last Tuesday. You were heading to the storeroom and you tripped but caught yourself on the shelving."

"That's because of those boxes you left on the floor. Anyone could have tripped over that mess!"

"There was nothing there that you hadn't walked past every day for the last year. You stumbled, Sam, and you know it, and it wasn't the first time," Pat said.

"Well, maybe you should put away that clutter, Pat. You do work here you know."

"Sam, I'm not saying they should put you down like an old racehorse. But what I am saying is, listen to Saul and face up to facts."

"I am 'facing up,' as you call it."

"Mmm-huh," Pat said as he took another sip of coffee.

The front door bells jingled and two police officers walked in. "Hello, Pop. Hey there, Pat. You got something for us?" one asked.

"Come on over here, Jerry. I've got it set aside," Pat said.

A young man with nervous eyes had come in the day before and hocked a brand new digital camera. "Let me see if it really works," Pat told him as he focused the camera and snapped a quick shot. Pat paid 20 bucks for the camera — mug shot included — and called the cops.

Pat was clever that way. He noticed things.

CHAPTER THREE

I maintained my independence for a while. Every month or so I visited Jeff's neurologist friend, Dr. Robinson, spending more time in his waiting room than with him. He gave me a prescription, and I'd stop in at Rudy Shellman's pharmacy on my way home to get it filled. I've known Rudy for years.

"Here you go, Sam," he said the day he filled the first one and handed me a small white paper bag. I must have had a sour look on my face because he leaned forward and whispered, "Hey, not so glum! Some of my customers get two or three bags a week. You're not in bad shape yet."

"Yet?"

Soon I was supposed to take one kind of pill in the morning and at night, and a different one every three hours — which was way too confusing. So I took them both every three hours. Jeff's eyes grew as big as Alka Seltzer tablets when I told him. So he got me a weekly pill case and sorted my medicine by day and time as if he were my mother packing my lunch. A pill case! Only old people have pill cases! But I reluctantly sorted the capsules myself every Monday afterwards.

"Here, Pop, I'll help you," he said the next time he came over and saw me filling the thing.

"I don't need your help," I snapped.

After that, he watched me like he did when he was a kid to make sure I wasn't snitching from his special jar of M&M's.

It wasn't long afterward that I had the wreck. Well, it wasn't exactly a wreck. It was a fender-bender. Well, it wasn't exactly that either.

I was driving home one afternoon listening to a talk show on the radio, noticed that the light was about to change and slowed down. What I didn't notice was the Range Rover in front of me that had come to a dead stop. By the time I did, I hit the brake pedal but couldn't press it down fast enough and BAM!

I put my car in park, removed my seatbelt and got out. The lady in the car in front of me got out a hell of a lot faster — all puffed up and ready for a shouting match.

"My fault, all my fault," I said as humbly as I could. She took a good look at me and another good look at her bumper and lightened up. The only damage on her car was a scraped bumper sticker that said, "What Would Jesus Do?"

A police officer arrived soon thereafter, looked for damages, checked my driver's license and handed it back. "Have you been drinking, Mr. Geller?" he asked.

"No, sir."

"Do you have a medical problem?"

I was so shaky trying to get my license back into my wallet that I decided to come clean. "I have Parkinson's disease."

"Sorry to hear that, sir. You should ask your doctor if it's safe for you to be behind the wheel. You could have hurt someone."

I could hurt someone?

"I will not give you a summons, Mr. Geller, because no one was hurt and there were no damages to the lady's car," the officer said. "Please be careful from here on out."

• • •

"You actually want to take the test?" the woman at the Department of Motor Vehicles asked later that day. "That's odd."

"I want to be sure that I'm a safe driver," I told her.

I had stopped by the DMV the day before to pick up a copy of the drivers' manual. I studied hard that evening and fretted like a 15-year-old. If I failed, my life would change. Everything would be more difficult. I'd have to depend completely on family and friends. But I wanted, actually needed, to prove to myself that I could do it.

That morning I walked carefully and deliberately into the DMV office — consciously lifting my feet so I wouldn't trip, measuring every step. I limited myself to one cup of coffee that morning so I wouldn't be too shaky. My head was packed with rules about vehicles passing on the right, which way to turn the wheels when parking on a hill, school bus safety, braking distances and parallel parking. I hadn't taken that test in more than 60 years! There weren't any interstate highways back then; there were hardly any paved roads.

The woman behind the counter recognized me from the day before.

"I'm here to take my driver's exam," I said nervously. It wasn't the Parkinson's that had me shaking that day.

She shrugged and directed me toward a computer, which was daunting in and of itself. Why does everything these days have to be on a computer? But I quickly figured it out, took the test and scored 88 out of 100.

"Your peripheral vision isn't the best," the woman said, "but you passed. That officer over there will conduct the driving portion."

I walked over to the officer and said I was ready to go. He looked at me, shook his head and asked, "Where's your car?"

I managed to stop when I was supposed to, use only my right foot on the brake and gas pedal, put on the correct blinker when turning and yield when the sign said yield. I didn't follow any cars too closely, and I maintained the speed limit and parallel parked without destroying the parking posts. The only thing I did wrong occurred after we arrived back in the parking lot. I got the switches mixed up for the power windows and door locks.

"Well, how did I do?" I asked the officer.

"You drive too slow but you passed," he said.

"You mean I can keep driving?" I asked nervously.

"Yes, but we'll need to take a photo of you to update your license. Put your toes on the red line in front of the camera and stand up straight. The lady over there will handle it."

"I am standing up straight," I said as the flash went off.

"How does this look?" she asked, showing me a picture of a wrinkled old man with thinning hair and a high shiny forehead because of the flash.

"Well, I guess that's about as good as I should expect," I said politely, wondering why Mr. T had not warned me earlier that morning that I looked like a goat from hell.

Pleased with myself, I returned to my car and left. I began paying closer attention to what I was doing. Didn't drive too slowly. Didn't drive too fast either. Didn't listen to the radio. I appreciated my car more than ever.

Over the past several years I've taken friends, including a few ladies, to movies, the symphony, weddings, bar mitzvahs and the like. "Oh, Sam, what would we do without you?" the ladies would always ask. I loved it.

Most of my social events revolve around my weekly card game with my buddies. "The Old Farts," we call ourselves, or sometimes just "the O.F.s." It started back when Sandy asked me where I was going on Thursday nights, and I said I was getting together with some old farts to play gin rummy. Not long afterward, a couple of the wives stitched together a banner for "The O.F. Club." Others try to guess what it means but never get it right. "Odd Fellows" and "Octogenarian Friends" are common guesses.

When together, we Old Farts give each other a hard time about the ways age affects us. "Are you playing cards or have you fallen asleep again?" or "Hey, Saul, your wife just called and asked that you stop by the drug store and get some Extra Strength Viagra on the way home," or "Good grief, Sam, why haven't you retired like the rest of us?"

When asked this question, I simply explained that single women come into the shop and flirt with me, keeping me young — which no one believes.

The O.F.s can be extremely irritating, each in his own predictable way. Abe Weiss has never gone an entire evening without asking, "Hey, Sam, do you get up at night to piss?"

"Oh, boy, here we, uh, *go* again," says Henry Levy, rolling his eyes. "Is there ever a night that we don't have to get up and take a leak? Can we skip the bathroom talk for a change?"

That's Abe's cue to bring forth the details of his entire 76-year urinary history, which lasts exactly 10 minutes and 36 seconds.

"I'll bet it's not clear anymore," Henry mutters just a few moments before Abe wraps up his exposé with, "It used to be clear but now it's yellow."

"Gee, imagine that," Henry always says, "just like last time and the time before that. Fascinating!" Then he adds, "Hey, I've got a great idea. Why don't we play some cards?"

That's when Saul serves everyone a glass of iced tea, which Abe refuses to drink because it makes him go to the bathroom.

Don't get me wrong. I love my friends. I've known most of them forever. But I still make new ones occasionally, and at my age that's not easy. When you go to as many funerals as I do now, it's nice to add to the list every now and then.

Speaking of making friends, Carol talked me into attending the monthly Movement Disorder Group meetings. Now, there's a name for you. At first I thought it had something to do with being constipated. "Why would anyone want to sit around and talk about that sort of crap?" I asked.

But she quickly straightened me out. "It's not that kind of 'movement.' It's for people who have trouble walking." "Movement disorder group" turned out to be a politically correct euphemism for a bunch of gimps. "The Stumble Bums" would be more like it.

Anyway, I felt like a king walking in on my own two feet at my first meeting. Most of them shuffled along, holding on tight to those waist-high walkers on wheels. The others used crutches or canes. One old guy drove a red motorized chair around the room as if he were cruising the Piggy Park Drive-In looking for chicks.

"That letch is rude and always in a hurry," a lady with a walker said after almost being run over by the man in the red Scooter Store rig.

Others complained about people being rude in general. "The Walk/Don't Walk signals at the intersections change too soon," one lady noted, "and those drivers will blow the horn if you don't get across in time. It's enough to give you a heart attack." She went on to say, "Steps are too steep, sidewalks are all curb and there aren't enough check-out lines in the grocery store."

"So stay at home!" I wanted to shout but didn't because she was obviously itching for a fight. Besides, it would have screwed up the quid pro quo: Each of them, it seemed, pretended to listen to another's problem for the sole reason of being entitled to an equal amount of complaining time. What a waste, I mumbled to myself after the meeting ended and I walked shakily out to my car, which I appreciated now more than ever.

But I went back to the next meeting of the Stumble Bums because I didn't have the heart to tell Carol how I really felt. "I'll give it just one more chance," I vowed.

At my second meeting I met Maurice Covington, a retired high school English teacher who wore perfectly round wire-rim eyeglasses and had a red beret and tweed sport coat with patches on the elbows. It was summertime and hot outside. Maurice walked in with his jacket over his arm and put it on after he entered the air-conditioned room. He sat next to me and didn't say much at first. He kept his hands pressed to the tops of his thighs. His fingernails were clean and neatly trimmed. Maurice and I soon became friends.

I later learned that Maurice had been divorced 10 years and remained single. His 16-year-old son, Philip, was — let me put it this way — slow. He lived with Maurice. Like my granddaughter, Philip required a lot of attention. Maurice said the boy could not be left alone under any circumstances, and his condition was complicated by seizures, although they occurred less frequently now.

Philip was physically able to attend public school but it was not easy, and Maurice was convinced that the teachers were unwilling to give Philip as much time and attention as other children. He might have been able to place his son in a school for children with special problems but decided it was best to home-school him.

Maurice had little time for anything else in his life. He retired early to care for his son, and played the roles of father, mother and teacher. I felt sorry for Maurice because I understood the strain he was under.

Maurice and I began a tradition of visiting the bar next door after the meetings and we often joked about our experiences with what we called the "Circle of Complaint." I kept going to the Stumble Bum meetings mostly to chat with Maurice afterwards.

Then I fell. Again.

Maurice and I were sitting in the bar talking about how exceptionally annoying the complainers had been that night. As I got up to leave, I pushed myself up holding onto the arm of my chair, lost my balance and down I went. I held out my hands to brace myself and snapped my right wrist when I hit the floor.

"Damn it," I said and stood up immediately. Lightening bolts of pain jolted my right forearm. It wasn't the Parkinson's that caused me to fall, I said to myself, but not so convincingly this time.

"Are you OK?" Maurice asked.

"I'm fine," I shot back. But I knew I wasn't. I was hurt. So then I added, "Damn it, no, I'm not OK, Maurice."

"You're not?"

"Can you get me to the Emergency Room?" I asked. "It's my wrist. Hurts like hell."

The waitress thought I had a stroke and called EMS. The last thing I wanted was to get strapped down in a gurney, hooked up to an IV and hauled away in an ambulance with sirens blaring.

"Come on, Maurice, let's go," I said.

He helped me out of the place and we walked what seemed like a mile to his car in the back of the parking lot. I crawled in as the ambulance arrived out on the street.

"Step on it!" I hollered.

He drove me straight to the emergency room, and as we pulled up to the big sliding-glass doors, he asked, "Should I call your son? Isn't he a doctor?"

"Heavens, no, don't call him, Maurice. He's a dermatologist. He works on warts, not broken wrists." Maurice helped me out of the car and through the doors where a nurse who looked like a drill sergeant was waiting with a rolling chair. I wondered if I'd ever walk back out. That's what happens when you're 80 years old and in a hospital emergency room.

It was after midnight when I did walk back out with a cast the size of a 10-pound dumbbell on my right wrist. It was a simple fracture and there was no need for screws. Maurice stayed with me the entire time. Both of us were exhausted when we arrived at my house. He offered to stay with me, saying he'd hired a babysitter for his son.

"Don't worry. I'm fine," I said as I thanked him and headed for the front door.

Getting in wasn't easy. My keys were in my right front pocket. Try reaching into your right pants pocket with your left hand and you'll know what I mean. I have missed my dear wife every day of the seven years she's been gone, but never as much as I did that night.

It took a while but I got the key out of my pants pocket and unlocked the door. I managed to get undressed down to my boxer shorts, brush my teeth and crawl into bed. But the pain pill they gave me at the hospital wasn't strong enough. I couldn't sleep.

Every position I tried made me ache even more. I started out on my back, then rolled to one side, then the other over and over again. I was miserable. I couldn't sit up. I couldn't lie down. I couldn't roll over any more. Not long before dawn, I finally managed to get a few winks as I sat like a condemned man in my favorite living room chair.

Jeff called early. Someone at the hospital tipped him off.

"What happened, Pop?"

"Nothing much. I'm OK," I said. But I was grateful that he called. I needed help.

Carol and Peggy arrived within the hour. Carol helped me dress and pack my bag for my move to their house. As she and I circled the room gathering up necessities, Peggy sat on the edge of the bed, staring ahead, her legs stretched out straight over the floor. Carol and I had to step over her feet as we moved around the room.

"Peggy, I appreciate you sharing your house with me for a couple of days," I said.

As usual she didn't answer, but her eyes followed me as I moved around the room.

"I'm only going to stay a few days until the pain eases up and I can take care of myself again."

"Stay as long as you need to, Pop," Carol said. "You know that."

Two months later it was obvious I was there to stay. Jeff and Carol had three "children" to care for now: Peggy, Kate and me. I had to adjust to living in a new place for the first time in 50 years.

CHAPTER FOUR

At Jeff and Carol's house I had my own room with a private bath and I felt comfortable and safe. Once it was clear that I wasn't leaving anytime soon, Jeff moved my bed and dresser and a few pictures over from my house. He also picked up my favorite chair. Mr. T moved in with me, too. He stood tall in their entry hall.

We left everything else in my house just the way it was. "Sure, Pop," Jeff said, when I said I'd be going back home eventually. "Whenever you're ready."

I continued going to work every day although I arrived late more often than usual. I knew Pat could handle it. He liked having more responsibilities. "Take the whole day off if you want," he'd say.

Not being able to drive while my arm healed was depressing, so I appreciated getting behind the wheel again and feeling like I was back in control. That's when I got a call from a local widow about my age named Irene Kurtz. A mutual friend told her I was going to the symphony and she asked me for a ride. So, of course, I agreed to pick her up. We talked and laughed continuously during the ride there, the intermission and the ride back to her house. I was giddy by the end of the evening.

As I walked her to her front door I said, "Anytime you need a ride, Irene, just let me know. Anytime. Just give me a call. Anytime."

She looked at me as if she were thinking, What is this old geezer getting at? My heart was racing when I got back into the car and I was wondering the same thing.

• • •

Maurice began picking me up for the Stumble Bum meetings after I broke my wrist, and these get-togethers became an important part of my social life. Of course, playing cards was essential, although I lost money more often than I won.

The Old Farts were concerned about my change of residence, but they understood. We knew people who insisted on living alone past the point they should have and were found dead on the floor.

"You've got it made," Henry said one night. "A pretty daughter-in-law doing the cooking, your son the live-in doctor and their children. Kids will make you young again!"

"When they're not driving you crazy," Abe said.

"Well, Henry, you're right about the cooking," I admitted. "Carol makes an incredible pound cake. I had some for breakfast this morning."

"Nothing wrong with that," Saul said. "You're 80 years old, why not?" That's one reason Saul is my doctor.

"But that bit about the live-in doctor isn't all it's cracked up to be," I continued. "If I have an outbreak of acne, having Jeff around would be great. But acne is not exactly my biggest problem right now. Have you ever seen anyone with acne at my age?"

Henry chuckled. "Well maybe you're right about that, but still, you should be proud of Jeff. He has done really well. And he knows more about the human body than you do!"

"I know what Sam means," Saul interrupted, stroking his chin, looking like the wise man he always yearned to be. "Dermatology is a limited specialty in the world of medicine," he joked. "But still, Sam, he was pretty quick to spot your Parkinson's."

"I am proud of my son, Henry," I said. "It's not easy to become any kind of a doctor." I threw down an ace and took a deep breath. I always get a queasy feeling when I talk about Jeff and his practice.

Why do I criticize him so often? I instantly regret doing so, but can't seem to stop.

"What's it like living with a teenager?" Henry asked, changing the subject. "It's been 40 years since I had to do it. I'm not sure I could go through that again."

"Kate's pretty good as far as teenagers go," I said, "but Peggy is another thing. When she screams, it's deafening. You never know when it's coming. No warning. It's ear-splitting."

Nobody said a word until Saul broke the awkward silence. "I'm surprised Carol hasn't found a cure for that yet. Seems like she's everywhere at once, volunteering for the cause," he said.

"You mean helping the retards?" Abe asked.

"No, Abe, I do not mean the retards, and you shouldn't talk like that. Makes you sound more ignorant than you really are," Saul said.

"That's hard to imagine," Phil Samet, the quietest Old Fart, muttered.

Saul continued, "I don't know how Carol does it. I know she works 24/7 helping those children — volunteering, lobbying, writing letters to the editor."

"Well, almost that much," I acknowledged. "She really cares and she won't give up. She feels called to help both the individuals affected by Rett's disorder and their families. I never truly understood how difficult these disorders could be on the entire family until

I saw it with Carol and Jeff and later with Kate. Thank goodness Carol has Rosetta to help her with Peggy now. She is a blessing."

Carol was a stay-at-home mom for Peggy's first five years. Jeff's practice grew quickly, so he could not be home as often as he needed to be to help Carol with Peggy. As Peggy got older, it was apparent to everyone that Carol needed help, even though she didn't want it at first. They eventually decided to hire Rosetta.

As Carol became more involved with supporting awareness of Rett syndrome, having Rosetta around was amazing. Now that Carol travels a great deal to support the cause, I don't know what we would do without Rosetta. She has developed her own relationship with Peggy and become part of our family. Rosetta can really connect and communicate with Peggy, which is something very few people can do.

"You know," Abe threw in, "I bet it must be tough on Jeffrey, his wife being so preoccupied. That's not good, if you know what I mean."

Phil nodded his head. "Yep. Yep. I know what you mean."

"Ya gotta wonder," Abe said. "There are so many temptations out there nowadays. Handsome doctor, wife's never home, wouldn't be the first time."

"What in the hell are you suggesting?" I snapped. "Is there something I should know? If there is, tell me! If not, mind your own damned business. It isn't like Carol is gone all the time! And how did we get on this subject, anyway?"

"Yeah, are we playing cards or listening to Oprah?" Henry asked. "Whose turn is it?"

Henry keeps us from crying in our beer — or he would if we drank alcohol, which most of the Old Farts can't tolerate anymore.

But Abe gave me more to think about that night than I wanted. What about Jeff? Could he possibly be having an affair? I had never even thought about it before, though I knew it was more common now than when I was young, and it wasn't exactly rare back then.

But why would he do such a thing? Was it difficult for him, having Carol gone that much? I felt sick. It didn't seem likely, and yet, I couldn't get it out of my mind. Truth was, I knew very little about my son.

My heart pounded like a pile driver. Why was I getting all worked up over something blowhard Abe Weiss said? I recalled the time he told us about a horrible crime involving kinky sex and murder that we later learned he had seen on an episode of "The Guiding Light." When we pointed out that a soap opera was not exactly a reliable source of news, he said, "Well, I saw it with my own two eyes! What are you guys, a bunch of professors or something?"

• • •

Maurice called one day to check on me. He was good about that. "I appreciate you not dying on me in the Emergency Room," he joked.

"Oh, you're welcome, my friend," I said. "I aim to please." We shot the breeze for a few minutes, talked about the weather, and then I asked him how Philip was doing.

"Oh, you know, he's fine," Maurice sighed. "I'd really hoped he'd be in college by now. Didn't turn out that way."

"I know what you mean. When they are born, you sit there and wonder what they'll be like when they get old enough to walk and talk. But then if you have a child like Philip or Peggy and they reach an age where they should be able to do those things but can't, it changes your whole perspective on the world. And we're lucky with Peggy. At least she can walk. Most people with Rett syndrome go their whole lives and can barely crawl, much less walk."

What an odd thing to brag about.

"You know, with all the monkey business politicians are into and the fickle way state budgets are put together, there's never enough money available for people like Philip and Peggy. All you have to do is read a newspaper to know that," Maurice said. "I wonder what will happen to Philip when I'm gone? Who will take care of him? Don't you worry about Peggy, too?"

"Come on, Maurice, it isn't like they would turn Philip out on the street," I said.

"You don't think so? You've seen the bag ladies and the bums sleeping under bridges. Most of them are mentally ill. How do I know the same thing won't happen to my son after I'm gone?"

"Surely someone would help him," I said. "That's one reason we pay taxes."

The thing that irritated Maurice the most was bureaucracy. At a meeting of the Stumble Bums a few days later, he started in on his rant.

"The cost of medical care is out of control," he said. "And those damned insurance people spend all of their time figuring out ways not to pay. They stall and stall, and they have the legislators in their back pockets."

Maurice was obsessed. "What would happen to people with disabilities if there were an economic collapse and they wound up out on the street?"

"Give it up, Maurice!" one of the other members of the group shouted when he asked basically the same question for the fourth time.

"No, he shouldn't give it up," a guest speaker replied. "This is something lots of people worry about. Unfortunately, there's no clear answer except that we should be finding a way to ensure that nobody has to worry about such things."

I guess I should have been more concerned about all this myself, but I felt that Jeff, Carol, Kate and I didn't have much to worry about. The pawnshop was worth something, especially since we owned the building, and Jeffrey was financially set. Besides, I had enough trouble just taking care of myself. I couldn't take on the health-care industry, too.

One night after getting home from the Gimp Class — that's another name Maurice and I had for it — the house was strangely quiet. Jeff was gone, again, and I thought about what Abe was intimating.

Damn Abe Weiss. He should mind his own business!

Carol was washing dishes and Kate was on the back porch gabbing on her phone as usual.

"Where's Jeff?" I asked as I walked into the kitchen.

"At the office catching up on paperwork."

"He sure works long hours," I said, careful to note her reaction.

"Most people don't know the number of hours doctors put in. If they did, they wouldn't be so critical."

"Right," I said, wincing because I'm one of the critics.

I walked out into the hall to Mr. T and took a look. The Hunchback of Notre Dame stared back at me. I tried to stand straighter. I could pull it off in the mornings but by nightfall I was hopelessly Quasimodo. I headed for the stairs.

Halfway up at the middle landing I almost tripped and fell. I was focused on the banister, which I held white-knuckled as I pulled myself up the steps. I didn't see Peggy sitting there until I ran into her. But there she was, her legs drawn up against her chest, her hands clasped, one on top of the other tapping repeatedly. She looked straight at me, following me with her eyes as if she wanted to tell me something.

"Oh, hi, Peggy," I said after I regained my balance. "Sorry. I didn't see you sitting there."

As usual, she did not speak, but I noticed just the beginning of a smile. I felt a great weariness, as if someone had tossed a heavy blanket over my shoulders. I sat down on a step, my feet on the landing next to her. She sat there with drool on her lower lip.

I remembered that my pillow was wet this morning when I woke up. I must have been drooling in my sleep. That's when something very strange happened. I looked directly at her and she did not scream. She actually looked back at me, but only for a moment.

"It's you and me, Peggy," I whispered. She continued to follow me with her eyes.

I rose awkwardly, struggling to keep my balance, holding onto the banister tightly. I went on up the stairs, stopped and looked back at her. Her hands were no longer clenched. She seemed relaxed.

Although Peggy can't talk, she does make a grunting sound from time to time. I suppose that is her way of communicating with the rest of us. The funny thing is, Rosetta understands what Peggy is trying to say. I don't know what it is between those two, but they make sense to each other.

A child who can't speak is pitied, avoided and often forgotten. I was guilty of having all three emotions with Peggy. Until that night on the stairs, there was no real bond between us. I had wondered occasionally what she was thinking or what she wanted us to do for her. But I never had a clue.

Sometimes she gestures, purses her lips or wrinkles her forehead. I began to take notice of these things and decided she might understand more than we think. If Peggy is upset, Rosetta places her hands on Peggy's shoulders and the screeches stop. For a long time, I've wondered what that was all about but never gave it much more than a passing thought. I began going with Carol and Peggy to her weekly physical therapy appointments. There I noticed how others with similar problems seemed to be interested in her. Were they communicating?

Then I got to thinking maybe we don't understand Peggy because we are so dependent on mere words. Instead of trying to bring Peggy into our world, we should figure out a way to enter hers. When I was a child, Doctor Dolittle was my favorite character because he talked to animals. I wanted to be like him. One day I looked straight into our pet terrier's eyes and said, "Look, if you understand me, wag your tail. No one will know. It'll just be you and me." And that dog wagged her tail! I'd forgotten all about that until the night I tripped over Peggy on the stairs.

That night as I was lying in my bed thinking, images of those birds — the ones Sandy, Jeff and I fed on the beach — filled my mind. Somehow they knew we were there and willing to share our crumbs. They somehow decided as a group to enter our world and all we could do was marvel.

CHAPTER FIVE

I'd be out of business if I didn't open the pawnshop on Saturdays, our busiest day of the week. Sales quadruple. Many customers bring in their payroll checks to be cashed then. I don't see how my grandfather and my father made it.

I sell more on Saturdays than Pat does, and that's very important to me. I enjoy outselling him. So I had mixed feelings when Jeff called on a Saturday not long ago and asked me to join him for lunch.

"Today?" I asked. "Just stop by the shop and we'll have lunch right here."

Jeff sighed. I could hear him. "No, Pop. It's a beautiful day. Let's get sandwiches and walk over to the park, OK?"

"That's fine," I said. "I'll call the deli. What do you want, chopped liver on rye?"

He laughed. "No, Pop, not chopped liver. I'd like a turkey sandwich on white, American cheese, lettuce and tomato."

"Got it. Some deli mustard, right?"

"Just a little, and mayo."

Surely Jeff heard *me* sigh this time. How could I have raised a son who likes mayonnaise more than mustard and turkey on white bread rather than chopped liver on rye? Giving up Shabbat is one thing. This is quite another. Is there no limit to assimilation?

"OK," I said as I finished giving my order. "And you'll deliver it in 10 minutes, right?"

"You're going out to lunch? On a Saturday?" Pat asked before I put the phone down.

I shrugged. "Jeff wants to talk about something. Carol probably put him up to it. Hope it won't be the assisted-living conversation."

"Assisted living?"

"It's coming, you know. Somebody has to look out for me as I fall apart, and it shouldn't have to be Jeff and Carol."

"You're not falling apart," Pat said. "Besides, if Jeff wanted to have that conversation, it wouldn't be on a Saturday. It would be on a Monday or Tuesday, don't you think?"

I looked at Pat and thought for a second. "You know me better than my only son, Pat. Why is that?"

"Because I spend more time with you than he does. I spend more time with you than anybody does. We're like an old married couple."

"God forbid," I said.

But he is right. We do spend most of our time together. He's a great partner.

I wished that I knew my son as well as I did Pat. My relationship with Jeff was polite and non-confrontational, which isn't much of a relationship at all actually. When we did talk, it was seldom interesting. Our conversations were stilted, always empty.

Jeff never seemed as if he needed me very much. He never asked for help with his homework, never sought my advice, never asked about girls or dating or anything like that. Maybe he talked to Sandy about those things. I don't know.

When my older friends talk about their children, it's usually about their problems. Henry Levy's son got kicked out of the Army, moved to Arizona and never came back. Irene Kurtz's granddaughter is a single mother with five children. Irene never mentions any other grandchildren. Maybe she doesn't have any. I decided to ask because I was looking for a good excuse to call her.

The bells on the pawnshop door jingled and in walked Jeffrey. He hadn't been inside the store in months.

"Dr. Jeffrey Geller!" Pat said from across the room. "Long time, no see!"

Jeff squinted toward the counter, where we both sat. "Hey, Pat. Couldn't you guys spring for some brighter lights? It's like a cave in here."

"No one else complains," I said. "Come on back. I'll call the deli and find out what's taking so long."

But before I could pick up the phone, David, the deli owner's son, was at the door with our lunch. "Sorry I'm late, Pop," he said. "They screwed up the order. When they saw two sandwiches for you, they assumed both were supposed to be chopped liver. They said you've never ordered anything but that. But I got it fixed," David smiled as he placed the bag on the counter.

"Thanks. How're your folks?" I asked.

"Good, good. Dad sends his best," David said and headed back out the door.

"Hey, Pop!" called Jeff from halfway across the room. "Aren't you going to pay?"

"Your father has an account," David laughed. "And he's the only one who has one."

Jeff looked surprised standing there in his yellow slacks and pink polo shirt with an alligator logo on the front. How could we be related? He's so country club…so Rockefeller.

Jeff walked up to the counter and asked Pat if he could spare me for lunch. "Can you handle the crowds?"

"No problem," Pat said.

"Don't forget to call the customer who phoned earlier about the lawnmower," I reminded Pat.

"Sam, I got it," he said. "Now get outta here! Enjoy yourself!"

Jeff and I walked about a block in awkward silence. We turned the corner and I nodded to Herb Walker, the lawyer, who was crossing the street. He looked like the million bucks he got paid for winning a recent libel suit against the ex-mayor. Herb represented Joe the barber, who sued the mayor for taking out an ad in the local paper the day after he lost the election that said: "Joe Mooney is a Political Hack." The ex-mayor was fighting mad about the haircut Joe gave him the day before the election; he said it was part of a conspiracy to make him look bad.

"I saw some brass knuckles in a box on the shelf of the shop," Jeff told me. "Sell many of them?"

"Nah, just a curiosity item. We stopped carrying brass knuckles. Didn't want to contribute to the delinquency of minors," I said with a wink.

Jeff smiled. He remembered the brass knuckles from years ago. He was in middle school and got into fight with the Webster brothers, bullies who enjoyed pushing skinny kids around. Jeff came home from school one day with a black eye and a torn shirt.

"What happened?" I had asked.

"Aw, nothing," he said.

So I let it drop. Fighting in school was common back then. The coaches would give the boys boxing gloves and tell them to settle their differences in the gym in front of the entire student body. It was part of the "toughening-up" process, they said. Can you imagine that happening today?

Anyway, a few days later the coach found out about the scrap and set up a rematch. He told Jeff he'd have to take on the Webster brothers one at a time. So Jeff asked me why he had to fight them at all, adding, "I'll get creamed!"

I didn't know what to say other than, "Let me think about it, son."

The next day when I was out of the store on an errand, Jeff walked in and bought a pair of brass knuckles from Pat. We sold a few back then even though it was against the law to actually use them. Pat told me, of course, and Jeff confirmed that he bought them.

"It's illegal, Jeff," I said. "It's like stepping into the ring with a baseball bat in your hands. If you break a jaw or bust a rib, you'll be in very serious trouble."

Jeff said he understood and went to his room. I hate to admit this, but I forgot about it. Then, all these years later as we walked to the park, it dawned on me that I should have asked him about it.

"What ever happened about that boxing match you were supposed to have with the Webster boys?"

Jeff grinned. "Don't you remember?"

"No."

"Well, I took those brass knuckles to school, even though you told me not to, and showed them to Charlie Webster, the youngest one. I threatened to tell the coach the knuckles belonged to them and told him I knew that the coach wouldn't allow us to fight after hearing that because he wouldn't want to be accused of contributing to the delinquency of minors. Charlie fell for it — told his brother to tell the coach that all three of us wanted to call the whole thing off, which his brother did, and the coach agreed."

"No kidding!"

"I feared for my life," Jeff said with a laugh. "The irony is Charlie Webster was so impressed I had a set of brass knuckles he became my pal. Not long before we graduated I gave him the brass knuckles as a gesture of friendship."

"You're brilliant, Jeff. You always were a smart kid."

I love the smell of chopped-liver on rye with a slice of sweet onion on top and a pickle on the side. Reminds me of my grandmother and her kitchen.

"Want a bite, Jeff? It's really, really good."

"No thanks, Pop," Jeff said as he held up his turkey and cheese on white with mayo oozing out the sides. "Want some of mine?"

"No way."

We sat side by side in the shade eating our sandwiches in silence.

"Pop," Jeffrey said. "We need to talk."

CHAPTER SIX

I listened carefully to what my son was saying this time.

"I'm worried, Pop. It's Peggy," he said.

"What happened?"

"Nothing yet. But her needs are more than we can handle — especially Carol because she does most of the work. Truth is, Peggy is an adult now and caring for her is extremely difficult both physically and emotionally. It is so hard on Carol."

"Is that what Carol says, that it's too much for her?"

"No. She would never say that, but she's obviously stressed, always tired. She says she sleeps OK, but that's not true. She's up most of the night pretending to read. She's unusually irritable — gets upset at little things and always 'has a headache.' I know I should do more, but I work hard to support all of us — especially Peggy. Anyway, we just got word that a room is available at the Shuler Center and Peggy is next on the list. You know about the Shuler Center, don't you Pop?

I didn't know what to say. So we sat there on the bench in silence for a while.

"You're going send Peggy off to a residential center?" I finally asked.

"What do you think, Pop? Carol and I need your opinion. This is the biggest decision we've ever had to make. What do you think

Kate would say? And Rosetta, too? But most importantly, Pop, what do you think we should do?"

"Well," I said, thinking I could not let Jeff down again.

For some reason I couldn't get anything to come out for a moment, which seemed like an hour.

"I appreciate you asking for my advice, Jeff. You know and I know that it's ultimately your decision — yours and Carol's. But I've been meaning to tell you about something. It happened just the other night between Peggy and me."

"What's that?"

"Well, I don't know exactly how to explain it other than to say I think Peggy and I communicated. We actually communicated, son. We looked at each other eye to eye and she did not scream."

"Pop, I don't know about all that. You know how limited she is."

"We were on the stairs. She was sitting on the landing and I was struggling to get to the top. I didn't see her at first. I tripped over her actually and almost fell. That's when she looked at me and I looked at her — it was for only a second or two — and we connected. It was the most amazing thing."

"She hates to be stared at," Jeff said.

"I know. I've seen how people gawk at her, and it's not mere curiosity. They look at her with disgust sometimes and she has to know it. It bothers me that they do that."

"Like she's an FLK," Jeff observed.

"Yeah," I said. "Like that."

When Jeffrey was in medical school he and his friends referred to children with undiagnosed developmental disabilities as FLKs, which stood for Funny Looking Kids. They even called each other FLKs from time to time. If one got a bad haircut, the others teased him. "You look like an FLK," they'd say. Big joke back then. Not funny now.

"You know, Jeff, I've never thought of Peggy that way. Peggy is Peggy, my special granddaughter. But something extraordinary happened between us on the stairway. There's not as much distance between us now. She still won't let me come too close, but I feel as though I can communicate with her and even understand her in a small way. It's very strange."

"Really?"

"Really. I can sit closer to her now, but not too close. A wall is still there. I kind of look off to one side, yet still see her through the corner of one eye, and she looks back at me the same way. We did that in the breakfast room for almost an hour the other day."

Jeff nodded his head and I continued.

"Peggy has made us all change," I told him. "She's taught me a lot about having patience. And Kate has learned from her too. Kate has become a very caring person thanks to Peggy, and that's saying a lot about a teenager. They're so critical of others, especially those who are different. I'll miss her if we put her in the Shuler Center. But she won't be alone there. She'll have care specialists 24/7 who know how to help her better than we do, especially the older she gets."

Jeff remained silent as I considered the question some more. While I wanted Peggy to stay, that seemed unfair to her parents. They've worked with her year after year, unable to take vacations, having little time to enjoy themselves. I can't imagine what it's like having to change a 25-year-old woman's diapers every day. Jeff and Carol deserve a break.

"I don't know what to say, Jeff. I appreciate your asking my advice, but this is a lot to take in all at once. I need some time to think about this."

"It's OK, Pop. We don't have to make a decision this minute," Jeff said. "Think about it for a while. We'll sit down together tonight after supper and talk — you, Kate, Carol, Rosetta and me. I have brochures and other information about the Shuler Center to show you. Carol and I want this to be a decision we make together."

Jeff wadded up the sandwich wrappers and picked up the empty soda cans and stuffed them into the bag. "Let's head back to the shop," he said.

"No, you go on home, Jeff. I want to stay here a while longer. I need to think." I looked up and tried to extend my right hand to give him a shake, but could hardly lift it. So I simply smiled.

"You sure you'll be OK?" Jeff asked, reminding me that Peggy wasn't the only FLK he was stuck with nowadays.

"Go on, I'm fine."

Jeff walked across the park looking like he was headed down a fairway in his pink shirt and yellow pants.

It is said that God does not give people more difficulties in their lives than they can handle. But He was pushing the limits with Carol and Jeffrey. Peggy has never had a chance to live a normal life. When she was diagnosed with Rett syndrome, we knew nothing of the disease. Few people did. Her doctors initially thought she had a rare form of schizophrenia, which they didn't know how to treat.

I often think about my interactions with Peggy over the years. I remember asking her when she was a child, "Peggy, don't you want some dessert?" as I held up a slice of cake. She said nothing. It was so frustrating. It was as if she wanted to make me angry. I thought at the time what she needed was a good spanking.

The doctors recommended that Peggy be given tranquilizers and sedatives, but Carol and Jeff were reluctant to try these. Peggy was almost 15 when Carol and Jeff put her in a day-care facility that offered classes for children with special needs. It was not an easy decision. Would the other children, many with behavior problems, harm her? The staff assured them she would be safe but her parents could not help but worry. Jeff and Carol have always wanted the best for Peggy. So they took a chance.

Not long after Peggy was enrolled, she came home with bruises on her thighs, buttocks and arms. Carol and Jeffrey were told Peggy had fallen down. But a few days later Peggy came home with welts on her shoulder and chest, and her eyes were swollen. Jeff and Carol went to the facility immediately and demanded answers.

"She must have fallen or something," they were told. "You know she's not right."

Carol and Jeff notified hospital authorities. A staff physician examined Peggy and concluded that her injuries were not accidental. A week later, the center's assistant director called Jeff and said the abuser had been fired.

Jeff was relieved, but Carol had questions. What exactly did the woman do to Peggy? Was there evidence? What did she hit her with: a hairbrush, a broomstick, fists? Carol wanted to know everything, every detail. Was Peggy her only victim? Peggy couldn't tell us. In a way, that was the hardest part. We never really knew.

"We should have never sent her there to start with," Carol kept saying.

Jeff and Carol filed criminal charges against the woman but she never went to trial. After a year and a half of "examining the case," the district attorney sent them a letter saying he would not prosecute. "I don't take cases I know I can't win," he wrote. In other words, he was more concerned about getting votes than serving justice.

Carol turned her furor into political action. She contacted every elected official who had any degree of responsibility: the mayor, city council members, state legislators, disability board members and directors. She sent letters and e-mails. She left messages, made appointments, spoke directly to as many authorities as possible.

She befriended local newspaper reporters and editors — knew them on a first-name basis. She established herself as a primary source for information about people with autism, Rett syndrome and similar problems. She didn't hold back when describing how people with mental disabilities were treated.

Her kitchen was her office at first. Notes, newspaper clippings and bound government reports covered the table and countertops. She spread out into the family room and then the master bedroom. She replaced the television set with a computer station. She bought a printer and a fax machine. She became a parent advocacy group organizer — a full-time lobbyist who never gets paid. She spoke to parents, groups, civic clubs and anyone else who would listen.

From then on, Peggy stayed home day and night. Carol trusted no one except family members and Rosetta with the care of her daughter.

CHAPTER SEVEN

When Sandy was alive I used to drive straight home after work, but since she's been gone, I figure what's the hurry? Since I've moved in with Jeff and Carol, the last thing I want to do is get in their way. So usually after work I take a stroll, chat with friends and generally kill time. Sometimes I drive over to Maurice's house. He has become increasingly despondent about his son and I worry about my fellow Stumble Bum.

That Saturday afternoon about an hour before closing time, I didn't say anything to Pat, grabbed my car keys and headed for the door.

"Sam, what's up?" he shouted across the room. "Don't you want to add up the receipts?"

"Sorry, Pat. Can you take care of it today? Walter will be here soon. He'll keep an eye on things while you do the tallies."

Walter Fraser is our security guard. He's even older than me. He used to hang out around the store when he was young and my father liked him. The shop had been robbed twice within two months, so Dad decided we needed a security system. I was thinking window bars and sirens; Dad handed Walter a badge and a policeman's hat that we had in stock and announced that he was our new security system. Dad paid him $25 dollars a week.

Walter arrives around closing time and walks along with Pat or me up to the bank to make the daily deposit. Walter loves his job.

He still stands tall like a combat soldier, plays the part well. We haven't been robbed since he started all those years ago.

"No problem, Sam," Pat said. "Where you going?"

"It's a family emergency," I said, sounding more ominous than I had intended.

"Is that why Jeff stopped by earlier?"

"Well, as a matter of fact it is. We're worried about Peggy," I said.

"Oh," Pat said and just looked at me.

People don't ask much about Peggy. They don't know what to say. Most have never heard of Rett syndrome. All they know is Peggy has a problem.

I waved goodbye to Pat and walked out the door thinking that after all these years, Rett syndrome is still a mystery. When Peggy was diagnosed, no one knew the cause. Jeff and Carol heard lots of theories: a vitamin deficiency, brain chemicals out of balance, a vaccine did it, something was in the water, medication Carol took during pregnancy. Jeff and Carol tried all sorts of treatments — all very expensive and all for naught.

Jeffrey meticulously tracked Peggy's symptoms for years trying to make sense of it. Peggy couldn't speak; her spine was bent; she could hardly walk. Her feet were splayed and she dragged one of them. She always hung her head like she was ashamed. She had difficulty swallowing, and as I said, she screamed. Nothing added up. Was Peggy in pain? Was she scared? Angry? She certainly couldn't explain why.

Jeff said there's a gene that determines whether or not one has the disorder.

Peggy's eye coloring is the same as my wife's — beautifully brown with flecks of gold that sparkle when the light is right. Sandy loved that child. She did all she could to comfort her. I wonder what Sandy would have said about sending Peggy off to the Shuler Center.

I didn't know how to respond to Peggy for years. I'd buy presents for her birthdays and occasionally attempt to give her a hug. But as soon as I got within 10 feet, she'd scream. So I stayed out of her way. I didn't know what to do.

• • •

When I got back to the house I was surprised to see Kate and Jeff sitting on the couch and thumbing through magazines as if they were in a waiting room at the doctor's office.

Kate was usually upstairs listening to music through headphones or talking to friends on her cell. A month before, she stopped by the pawnshop to get some things for a school art project. She was creating a sculpture of "found objects," she said. What better place to look than your grandfather's pawnshop, right?

"That's fine with me," I said.

She selected two spark plugs, a lawnmower blade, a socket wrench, a fishing rod and a mannequin, which was in the front window. "Pop, this shop is so cool!" she said.

"Yes, it is," I said. "Especially when you are here."

I remember the time she became fascinated with make-up — really garish stuff all her friends were using. She arrived at the dinner table one night wearing bright blue and purple eye shadow and one lip black, the other green.

"Have you been in an car accident?" I teased. "Want me to take you to the emergency room?"

She pretended that she didn't hear me.

"Were there any survivors?"

Still no response.

One day she announced that she was joining the Peace Corps. She spread out maps of the whole world and highlighted the Amazon rain forest. "What kind of stuff do I need to know to help people who live there, Pop?"

Twice she went on a vegan diet, which was agonizing. And she raved about rock bands with names like "The Red Hot Chili Peppers" and "Smashing Pumpkins" — all of which sounded like a bad case of indigestion.

Jeff and Kate looked up as I walked into the living room and they said hello distractedly, before resuming their reading. I headed to the kitchen where I knew the welcome would be warmer. Carol was baking fresh bread and the countertop was covered with vegetables. It looked like a farmers' market in there.

"Hi, Pop. You hungry?" she asked. She stood at the sink rinsing off tomatoes.

"We having guests for dinner?" I kidded.

"No. We're having a healthy dinner for ourselves."

"You fix one every night," I pointed out, "but I'm not complaining."

"It's wonderful to have at least one person around who appreciates it," she said.

"Want me to chop some onions? Snap some beans?" I asked.

"Oh, no, Pop, that's … " she started to say, then changed her mind. "That would be nice, Pop, thanks."

I pulled a carving knife from the drawer and stood ready to take orders. Carol gently took the knife from my hands, gave me a shorter one, led me to the cutting board and said, "Start with a bell pepper."

It took me a while to slice it the way she wanted and by the time I was through she had removed the bread from the oven and inserted an apple pie — a store-bought apple pie, which was odd for her.

"So how was your day?" I asked.

"I took Peggy to the grocery store and she wandered off when I was trying to read a label."

"Oh?"

"She started screaming in the next aisle, knocked over a soup can display and soiled her diaper. I didn't get a chance to get the chicken because I was in a hurry to get her calmed down and out to the car and couldn't make it through the checkout line. But the store manager followed us out and handed me a bag of the food that was in my cart. She said she stuck an apple pie in there for dessert and that I could pay her later. So tonight we're having garden-fresh salad and store-bought pie, which is just as well because I'm worn out, Pop."

I took Carol's hand and squeezed it.

The front door opened and Rosetta walked in saying Peggy was home and her pants were wet.

To my surprise, Kate jumped up off the couch and said, "Come on, Peggy, I'll help you." Kate reached out for her older sister, who recoiled as usual. Kate continued walking to the staircase urging Peggy to follow her. Finally, with Rosetta nudging, Peggy did. Kate climbed the stairs and began talking up a blue streak.

"So how's your day been, Peggy? I heard you went to the store with Mom, right? You guys were out of the house before I woke up this morning. When I came downstairs the place was empty and I didn't know…."

Kate bathed her sister in words, never waiting for a reply. I never noticed this before, but thinking about it now, I realize that she's always done this. I admire Kate for trying. It hasn't been easy for her. Rosetta followed behind Peggy to help.

It seemed like just the other night when Kate attended her first prom. I stopped by on the way home to see her off. Jeff, Carol and I were sitting in the living room waiting for her boyfriend Michael to arrive.

Kate came downstairs but she was not smiling. Tears streaked her makeup. Her face was flushed like she had just run the Boston

Marathon backwards.

"Pop, I don't want Michael to come here!" she sobbed. "Why can't I just go to Barb's house? He can pick me up there. I don't want him here!"

It was obvious she was trying to draw me into an argument that had started earlier.

"What if Peggy lets out her crazy scream when he's here? I'll be so embarrassed!"

"Kate, just calm down," Carol said. "It'll be OK. Calm down. Getting upset will make it worse."

All of us knew that Carol was right. The more tension in the house, the more likely it was that Peggy would cut loose with a blood-curdling yell. I didn't blame Kate for not wanting her first prom night to start out that way.

"Mom, I can't calm down. How would you feel if you were in my shoes? She's uncontrollable!"

"Kate, this is your sister you're talking about," Carol said. "She can't help it."

"But, Mom! This is my prom!"

"Honey, Peggy is a member of our family. We don't hide any member of our family. We have no reason to be embarrassed. I know you are nervous about your prom, but it will not be the end of the world if Peggy gets upset."

Carol is a stone wall when she makes up her mind to be. Kate threw up her arms and stormed back up to her room. Michael arrived on time, Kate looked fine and Peggy did not scream. All that fuss for nothing — but it has been hard on Kate through the years.

• • •

Anyway, Kate, Rosetta and Peggy went upstairs and I heard Kate talking continuously.

"You want your blue bunny pants, don't you? They're pretty,

Peggy, don't you think? Remember the bunnies we saw at the pet store? They were so soft, don't you think?"

Peggy never said a word. She didn't scream either.

Later when we were seated at the dinner table, everyone seemed on edge.

"Pop made the salad and snapped the beans," Carol said.

Peggy fingered the vegetables on her plate, grabbed a slice of cucumber and put it in her mouth. She chewed a little, then took it back out and placed it beside her plate. Rosetta, who sat next to her, watched out of the corner of her eye.

I thought about the few times Jeffrey, Carol and Kate joined Sandy and me at our house for dinner. They left Peggy at home with Rosetta. Everyone relaxed for a change. It could be like that all the time if Peggy moved to Shuler, I thought.

Peggy babbled and drooled, pushed more food off her plate, tilted her head back and stared at the ceiling. Would Peggy miss us if she were sent away?

CHAPTER EIGHT

We were sitting tensely around the dining room table, trying to have some semblance of a normal meal, wondering what would happen to Peggy — should she go, should she stay?

Suddenly Peggy closed her eyes and screamed louder than ever. I covered my ears with my hands. Carol and Rosetta rose from their chairs in unison and reached over to comfort her.

Kate tried to calm her sister. "It's OK Peggy, it's OK. Nothing's wrong. Let's take a walk now. I'll walk with you."

I got up and headed for the kitchen as the others scrambled to help her. I stopped, turned and looked back at Peggy. She looked directly at me, and I back at her. She fell silent for only a second or two, and through her tears she spoke to me again without saying a word — like that time before on the stairs.

Rosetta held out her arm and Peggy grabbed it. They went to her room. The rest of us cleared the table in silence. We knew we had a lot to discuss regarding Peggy's future.

"What happened?" Jeff asked Carol.

"I don't know, Jeff!" Carol shouted. "I don't know any more than you do!" It wasn't often that we heard Carol raise her voice.

"We need to talk," Jeff said.

Rosetta remained upstairs with Peggy while the rest of us gathered in the living room. Jeff and Carol sat beside each other on the big couch, Kate picked a spot on the small sofa and I sat in my recliner. Jeff cleared his throat and began to speak.

I'm glad the two of you are here," he said, looking at Kate and me. "Carol and I appreciate it. We need your help in deciding what to do. Maybe what happened tonight was a good thing. Maybe it puts everything into perspective. It's only going to get worse, you know."

His voice broke. He cleared this throat again and looked at each of us.

"Carol and Rosetta have worked so hard to help Peggy, to comfort and care for her all these years. But I don't think they can do that anymore. I don't think any of us can continue the way we're headed, and we won't be around forever to help Peggy. Someday we'll be gone. Pop, you're 80 years old, for God's sake. And Katie, you've got your own life to live whether it is in the Amazon with the Peace Corps or married with children somewhere. Carol and Rosetta and I will be gone some day, too.

"Peggy must have constant care. She cannot make it on her own. She will have to live somewhere else eventually. Maybe that time is now."

"Now?" Kate asked. "You're talking about right now?"

"We haven't decided anything yet, Katie," Carol said.

"But Mom, I don't want Peggy to leave us now. I'll stay home and look after her. I don't have to go off to school, you know. I'll help you. Peggy's my sister and I love her. She doesn't embarrass me anymore. Please don't send her away."

Jeff and Carol looked at each other and then at Kate.

"Katie," Carol said quietly. "We know you love your sister and we know you aren't embarrassed by her anymore. We also know that you are sincere when you say you're willing to stay home and care for her. But you have your own life to live. We want you to go off to college and prepare yourself well to fulfill your dreams."

No one said anything for a few moments. Then Jeff, Carol and Kate turned toward me. It was my turn to speak.

"Well," I said, not knowing what would come next. "Uh, I think part of the problem is me. Perhaps I'm the one who should leave and move into an assisted-living home. I'm old and we all know I'm going to need more and more help with little things. Henry Levy moved into one of those places last month. It's called 'Sunnyside' or something bright and cheery like that. It's brand new."

"This is not about you, Pop," Carol said. "Jeff and I are trying to figure out what's best for Peggy. You're no problem. We want you here with us. We need you."

I attempted to say something, to say I loved and needed them too, but the words would not come. Rosetta slipped quietly into the room at that point and sat down across from me, beside Kate on the sofa.

"Peggy has been accepted by the Shuler Center," Jeff said. "It's the best care facility in town. It has a waiting list, and it's a long one. Some folks have been on it for years hoping to get their loved ones in. We won't get another chance. Today is Saturday. We have to tell them what we are going to do on Monday. If we decide Peggy should go, we will move her in two weeks."

Jeff looked at his youngest daughter and asked, "Katie?"

"This is her home. She's fine right here. She'll never adjust to living anywhere else."

"Katie," Carol said. "It's not like we'd just send her away and never see her. We can go to the Center and we can take her out. We can bring Peggy here for meals or whatever we want to do."

"Like visiting hours?" Kate asked.

I sat nervously, afraid Jeff would call on me again.

No one said anything for a while. The only sound came from the grandfather clock out in the hall next to Mr. T.

Jeff looked at me and I looked down at the floor. "Pop, what do you think?"

The Shuler Center was only 15 miles away — I drove by it often — but at that moment I felt as if I were being asked to pack Peggy's suitcase and send her into outer space. No words came from my mouth. I just sat there shaking like an old man with Parkinson's disease.

"I don't want her to go," I blurted out. "Maybe Katie is right. Maybe she won't be able to adjust anywhere else."

Maybe before my Parkinson's became noticeable, I would have felt differently. Maybe a year ago I would have been more rational. But my relationship with Peggy had changed. I did not want her go. Something special was happening. I was breaking through to her.

"Pop," Jeffrey said. "None of us want her to go. But we must do what is best for all of us, including Peggy."

We all sat silently, each thinking what life would be like without Peggy here every day.

Kate broke the silence. "We can visit her?" she asked.

Carol nodded. "Of course. And she can visit us. She can't spend the night here because that would be too confusing for her once she's adjusted in her new home. But she can come over any day we want, and we can go there any day we want."

More silence, except for the clock ticking in the hall.

"And you both think this place is the best?" I asked.

"No question," Carol said. She'd done her research. Carol knew what she was talking about.

Rosetta spoke up. "My sister Martha, she works at Shuler. It's a nice place."

We all value Rosetta's opinion. She's been a part of our family for 20 years.

"Peggy is my child, too," Rosetta said. "She will be safe at Shuler. Martha will watch out for her, and I can be there too, making sure Peggy is clean, comfortable, well-loved and properly fed."

For two more hours we went back and forth on what to do with Jeffrey listing the plusses and minuses of the move. Carol poured tea. I paced, shakily. Kate and Rosetta listened carefully. It was 11 p.m. when we reached a conclusion. Peggy would live at the Shuler Center, probably for the rest of her life.

Rosetta went home and the rest of us went to our rooms. I slowly climbed the stairs as I turned everything over and over in my mind. I stopped at Peggy's door and peeked in at her sleeping. She sighed deeply. I wondered if she dreamed.

CHAPTER NINE

On Monday, Carol called the administrator at the Shuler Center and made the arrangements. Peggy would check in to her new home in two weeks. We didn't talk about it much. A sense of deep regret permeated the house. It felt like a funeral home. There was no happiness within those walls.

On Thursday at our weekly gin rummy game, I told the Old Farts what was happening.

"Jeff and Carol deserve a break," Saul said. "It's not healthy to be on call constantly like they have been for the past 25 years. I've looked into the Shuler operation and the place has an excellent staff. I know several of the doctors who call there. Peggy will get the best care."

"Look at it this way," Abe Weiss said. "You'll each have your own bathroom when she's gone. That's healthy too."

Henry shook his head. "You're so anal, Abe … uh, correction, make that *urinal*. You're so urinal, Abe. You're starting to piss me off as a matter of fact."

"Zip it and deal, Abe!" Phil shouted.

• • •

It was 6:30 p.m. the following Friday when I came down the stairs freshly shaved with a splash of Old Spice, in my khaki pants and a light blue, long-sleeve oxford shirt with a button-down collar and my well-broken-in brown leather loafers.

I walked past the big clock in the hall, stopped and said hello to Mr. T, who quickly reminded me that my belt buckle was out of line and my zipper was open. Mr. T is always honest, and on this particular evening it was very important that I look sharp.

Sandy used to say my khakis and blue oxford shirt were my "uniform" — and she often reminded me to polish my shoes.

"Loafers don't look right unless they have a fresh shine," she'd say.

Mr. T said the same thing too, so I stood on my left leg and rubbed the top of my right shoe up and down three or four times on back of my left pant leg, then I shifted my weight and shined the top of the left shoe on the back of my right leg. I couldn't shine shoes the way I used to. I can't bend over far enough to get to them. Khakis are perfect for this.

I never was a snazzy dresser. I couldn't figure out which colors went best with what. Should I wear stripes or solids? Paisley or squares? Light coat with dark pants, or the other way around? It got worse as I aged. None of my socks match anymore, and I often put them on inside out. So I play it safe, especially when stepping out. I always wear a light blue Oxford shirt and khaki pants and brown leather loafers. Oh, and I have a dark blue blazer, too, with gold-color buttons in case I'm going to an extra-special event.

I never wear a tie anymore and no one complains, which is good. It's not easy tying a tie when you're 80 years old and you have arthritis and Parkinson's disease. Fact is, I never know when I'll get the shakes. They come and go, and lately it's been more of the former and less of the latter. It's embarrassing, especially when attempting to drink anything. Lifting a cup of coffee or tea is like an eruption of Old Faithful, and the tremors are always on time — exactly when I don't want them. Mr. T reminds me of my situation, and Mr. T never lies. But I thanked him as usual that evening and pretended I did not care.

It was at that moment the back door slammed and Jeffrey walked in from the golf course. Jeff takes off early on Fridays to play with his friends. He moved quickly down the hall in perfect stride as if he had just won the Masters. He inherited his steady gait from his mother, not me. I walk like a drunk trying to keep a straight line. Stand on one foot and touch the tip of my nose with my hand? Forget it.

"Hey, Pop, what's up. You going out on a date?" He laughed and took two steps up the stairs. When I didn't say anything, he stopped and stepped back down. "You really are going out on a date, aren't you?"

I didn't say a word.

"Who is she, Pop? Will she pass inspection? That's what you used to ask me way back when." Jeff chuckled. "Seriously, Pop, do I know her?"

"Jeffrey, I'm 80 years old. What makes you think an old coot like me would return to the dating scene?"

"Don't be so modest, Pop. You can't fool me. All the widows in town have been calling you lately. You still got it, old man!"

"Got what?"

"You must have an aura that women your age cannot resist. Who you taking out tonight, Pop?"

"An aura, huh? Sort of like James Bond, maybe? I'm going to share something with you. I'm going to show you my secret weapon," I said. I reached down deep into my khaki pants pocket and pulled out my car keys. I held them over my head and jingled, which requires very little effort when you have Parkinson's.

"I can still drive and have a renewed license to prove it! Any man over age 70 who can still drive attracts more, uh, shall we say, 'experienced' women than a sultan keeps in the back of his tent."

• • •

It wasn't long after Sandy died that the phone started ringing and ladies I hardly knew were cooing on the other end of the line. They said they were sorry to hear about Sandy, asked how I felt, if I was lonely, if I was getting enough to eat. "You need to get out more, don't you think, Sam? It's not healthy to stay home by yourself."

So now I don't need to read the newspaper's calendar of events to know what's happening around town, I explained to Jeff as my keys continued to jingle. "The ladies keep me fully informed: 'There's a special opening tomorrow night at the art museum. Will you take me?' 'I just love the symphony, and I need a ride. You are going, aren't you?' 'I'd just love to go see that new Brad Pitt movie. We could go to the ice cream parlor afterward. Dutch treat?'"

I was flattered at first, pretending it was my good looks, refined manners, excellent conversational skills and finely tuned sense of humor that attracted them. But it eventually dawned on me that they were more interested in my wheels than my wit. What they really wanted was a ride.

"Women don't like staying at home, no matter their age," I told Jeff. "And they hate driving alone at night. You know, son, there's an old saying: 'In the land of the blind, the one-eyed man is king.' It's a great expression, don't you agree? Fact is, for women over 70 who live throughout this land, I reign supreme!"

Jeffrey smiled. "So pray tell me, Sire, who will his Majesty be escorting tonight?"

"Irene Kurtz. I've taken her out a couple of times already. She asked me over for supper. She's serving chopped liver."

Jeffrey rolled his eyes. "Doesn't sound like she needs a ride to me!"

"Chopped liver has been good to me, son. Before I met your mother I dated any Jewish girl I wanted. All I had to do is tell her mother that I just loved chopped liver and *bam*, just like that, I was asked to join the family for dinner. Chopped liver worked every time — and that was just for appetizers, if you know what I mean."

Jeffrey shook his head and grinned. "The way to a man's heart is through chopped liver? Is that what you're telling me?"

He chuckled all the way up the stairs.

After Sandy died, I was careful to socialize with women only in groups. I had no desire to be paired up. I had been married for almost 50 years and never really wanted to be with another woman.

Irene Kurtz was widowed 10 years ago after a long and happy marriage. She's financially secure, has lots of friends and enjoys a full social schedule. Sandy and I knew the Kurtzes casually. We'd see them at parties and community events, but we were never close. I do remember the sound of her laughter from back then, how her voice lightened everyone's mood.

I was glad Irene called me. She has a beautiful home. She likes bold, abstract prints, comfortable and modern furniture, and bright, cheerful rugs. She lives in a lovely neighborhood not far from Jeff and Carol's house.

"Would you mind fixing us drinks, Sam?" she asked soon after I arrived, and pointed to the marble kitchen counter on which were carefully arranged bottles of gin, tonic, glasses, a lime on a cutting board, a knife, a bowl of ice and silver tongs.

"Sure thing," I said. "But, uh, first I'd like to use your bathroom, please."

I was becoming like Abe, always worried about having to go. But Abe doesn't have Parkinson's. He doesn't know what it's like when you really, really have to go.

"Of course. It's down the hall, first door on the right," Irene said.

I was "relieved" in more ways than one.

I returned and fixed the drinks.

"Shall we get more comfortable, my dear?" I had said, which

sounded all wrong — like gigolo talk. I couldn't believe that I said it like that and began to blush.

"Wonderful," Irene said, which again put me at ease. "Why don't we move into the den? It's quite comfortable in there. I'm sure you'll like it."

"You're sure I'll like what?" I asked before realizing she might take it wrong.

"You'll see," she smiled warmly. She knew I didn't mean it the way it sounded.

We sat side by side on an over-stuffed red couch. We sipped our drinks and talked about a lot of things. She told me about her granddaughter Jennifer, who's in her 20s and lives near her parents in Virginia.

"Jennifer has a learning disability," Irene said. "She doesn't read or write well and her speech is different. She got a job through Social Services bagging groceries at a supermarket and met a young man there who handles the shopping carts. He brings them in from the parking lot, keeps them in good working order. They have a lot in common. They understand each other."

"That's wonderful," I said. "It's important to have someone special like that."

"Unfortunately, not everyone sees it that way," Irene said.

"Really?"

"The store manager spotted them holding hands in the parking lot after work. He called Jennifer's mother and complained — said it was bad for business and there was no telling what might happen. He said she might get pregnant, adding that retards should not be allowed to get too friendly. He called my Jenny a retard!" Irene said.

My first thought was to get in the car, drive to Virginia, find the store manager, remind him that Jennifer and her boyfriend are human beings who deserve respect, and then proceed to wring the man's neck.

"They should be able to share each other's company — just like you and me," I said.

Irene nodded.

"When I was a young man, I learned something very important from my father. An old man stopped in one day and asked if he could pawn a pair of pants. No one else would have given them a second look. They had no value. I brought my hand up to my face and almost burst out laughing. But my father treated him with respect. He waited on him as if he were the richest man in America.

"'How much do you want for these britches?' my father asked him.

"'I'd like to have $3 dollars, Mr. Geller.'

"My father reached into his pocket and handed him three one-dollar bills. He gave that man a lot more than money that day. He gave him respect. My father then turned to me and said, 'Remember the Golden Rule, son, and the world is a better place.'"

As I spoke those words, Irene reached over and took my hand. "You're a good man, Sam Geller. You're a very good man."

Irene looked into my eyes intently for a few seconds, stood up and nodded toward the kitchen. "There's chopped liver in there waiting for you."

We've talked about a lot of things since that night and haven't stopped talking since. We get together once or twice during the week, and I don't think Irene would mind if I tell you: No matter your age, or how achy and shaky you are, you're never too old to fall in love, and doing so requires no written instructions. The sparks still fly if you let things happen naturally. And I don't think she'll mind if I tell you that I stay over at her house when I'm too tired to drive home. She has a lovely guest room....

CHAPTER TEN

I've had a more positive attitude about life since I've been seeing Irene. When I think of her as I walk through the park, I pick up my pace a little, and I sleep better, too.

"Sam, what's gotten into you?" Pat said one morning at the shop. "You've got more spring in your step. Did Saul change your prescription?"

"I'm glad to be alive," I said and left it at that. I like to keep Pat wondering.

I've accepted the fact that I have Parkinson's disease and it will not go away — that it affects my brain and my signals get crossed at times; that my muscles are shutting down; that I drool occasionally and have difficulty swallowing. The tremors will continue and one day, I might not be able to talk as easily as I do now. I know I won't get better.

I'm reminded of what my father told me not long before he died. He said that in the 1930s the Nazis passed a series of laws in Nuremberg restricting Jewish people's lives. Week after week things got progressively worse. Jews could no longer visit city parks; could no longer do business with Aryans; couldn't even leave their neighborhoods without written permission. It was one bad thing after another.

Parkinson's is like that. I'm slowly losing my senses. I never know what to expect. I'm too hot one day, too cold the next. I always carry a sweater with me now, even in August when the thermometer hits 100 degrees. My vision is blurred sometimes. I checked the cash register receipts the other day and couldn't read a thing. I haven't quit driving yet, but someday Jeffrey will confiscate the keys.

I go to Movement Disorder Group meetings hoping to hear there's something new that will help — a miracle diet, a super pill. Maurice no longer joins me there, not since the night he stood up in front of everyone and read a magazine article about the increase in medical-related suicides among Americans trying to cope with debilitating health problems.

"The bills keep going up. They're impossible for me to pay," Maurice said. "My insurance has run out and the bureaucrats who are supposed to help me do not return my phone calls. It's no wonder that people like me are killing themselves."

A woman on the front row stood, pointed her finger at Maurice and scolded him. "You're talking crazy. Suicide is the work of the devil."

Maurice muttered, "People do crazy things when they're desperate," and walked out embarrassed. I excused myself and followed him outside.

"Maurice. You OK?"

He smiled cynically but said nothing.

"Look here, Maurice Covington, this nonsense must stop," I said. "You're obsessing about it, so knock it off."

He stood there with blank expression.

"Maurice, you need help."

"Well, Sam," he finally said. "I saw a shrink not long ago and she asked about my medications and my childhood and my ex-wife — all the usual stuff. She didn't tell me anything I didn't already know, so I never went back," he said, unnervingly agitated.

"Look, I'm a retired schoolteacher on a fixed income. I'm the only one who cares for my son, and it's expensive. I called the Department of Social Services about financial aid. I got a long list of names of people with long titles and phone numbers. But not one of them would talk to me. So I quit trying."

"Maurice, obviously you're depressed, and who wouldn't be under the same circumstances. But suicide? You aren't thinking of…of…."

"No, Sam, of course not."

That night, standing out there in the parking lot, Maurice looked so tired. He had been fighting the insurance companies, fighting the bureaucracy, fighting society. He was fighting with himself, too, and he was losing. He was convinced that he could no longer care for his disabled son and that no one would help him. He was giving up.

I know that's what Maurice was thinking as he stood there, his eyes half-closed, not looking at me — not looking at anything. He did not even blink.

I stopped talking. I'm a pawnshop owner, not a psychiatrist.

• • •

I called Irene as soon as I got back to the house that night. "Maurice has no family, except for his son Philip, who can't talk. Part of me says I should mind my own business. Another part says I should report Maurice to the authorities."

"You mean like call the police?" Irene said.

"If the police responded to every call like that, they wouldn't have time for anything else," I said.

"Sam. You have to do something, if not for Maurice's sake, then for Philip's sake, and if not for Philip's, then for yourself. What if something terrible happens?"

"What happens if I do call the police?" I asked.

"Nothing probably," Irene said.

"Yeah, I know. If I call the cops and tell them my friend is thinking about killing himself and maybe his son, too, they might think I'm the one who's crazy. They'll ask for proof: 'Does he have gun? Is he standing out on a ledge threatening to jump? What exactly do you expect us to do?' And the fact is, Irene, there's nothing anyone can do for him right now."

"It's late, Sam. Better sleep on it. We'll talk more in the morning."

I thanked Irene and hung up. The house was dark and dead silent. Carol went to bed early that evening after spending the day at the Capitol lobbying lawmakers to pass a bill halting "aversive treatment" for troubled children housed in state facilities.

Jeff was at the office as usual. I considered calling him about Maurice's odd behavior. Maybe he knew a psychiatrist who would see Maurice for free. Maybe Maurice needed "aversive treatment" instead of those poor children Carol worried about. Maybe Maurice should be locked in a padded cell.

Carol told me that some of the children are extremely difficult to control so they're locked in a "a time-out room." It's like solitary confinement at a prison, she said. Sometimes they bang on the walls. One child broke a finger recently doing that, she said.

I walked into the kitchen and the dishwasher was humming. Carol left me a note saying meatloaf, rice and vegetables were in the oven. I ate, cleaned up and climbed the stairs. I looked in on Peggy, who was asleep. I wondered what was going through her mind at that moment.

CHAPTER ELEVEN

Two days later, I woke early after a fretful sleep. I had two nightmares, one about Maurice and the other about Peggy — each was lost and alone and I couldn't find them. I managed to get dressed and went down the stairs into the kitchen.

Carol served my coffee and asked if I wanted eggs and lox.

"I'm not hungry. I've got a lot on my mind."

"What's wrong, Pop?" Carol asked.

"I'm worried about a lot of things … including Peggy."

"Me too," Carol said.

"I'm also worried about Maurice. He's been talking crazy. He's got suicide on his mind. I can't tell if he's seriously thinking about it or what. I know that sounds strange, but I had an odd conversation with him the other night night. He's so despondent."

Peggy sat at the table. Her head was down and turned to one side as usual. Her eyes were closed but she was not sleeping. I wanted to put my arm around her and tell her I love her but I was hesitant to get too close. I sat next to her looking straight ahead. I slowly turned toward her and she opened her eyes. She looked directly at me ever so briefly. I looked away, as did she. Then we looked back at each other for a few seconds, then away again.

"What are you two doing?" Carol asked.

"Oh, nothing." I said, but I couldn't help thinking that we were dancing.

After a few moments of silence, Carol asked, "Pop, Jeff and I are taking Kate on a shopping trip today. She needs new clothes for college. And we'd like to take her to supper. Rosetta is out of town visiting her son. Will you watch Peggy for us?"

"Well, sure," I said as I peeked over at Peggy again and she quickly looked up. It was almost as if she smiled.

Not long after Kate and her parents left, I called Maurice to check on him. I got his answering machine.

"Maurice, this is Sam. Please call me as soon as possible. I'm at Jeff's house. You have the number. I really want to talk to you, Maurice, so please call me."

I waited a while and tried again. I knew he was home.

"Maurice, I'm worried about you. Please return my call."

At about 4 p.m. the phone rang. I answered immediately.

"This is Alice Myers at Social Services. Is this Sam Geller?"

"It is. How can I help you?"

"Mr. Geller, you are the emergency contact listed on all the forms Maurice Covington filed with us regarding his son Philip. Have you spoken to Maurice lately?"

"Not since the night before last," I said. "He's very distraught. He's worried about his son. His insurance has run out."

"I know. I know. He called our office this morning and left an odd message. He said he has run out of options — then hung up. I called him but no one answered. I'm worried Mr. Geller, but I'm out of town and can't get to his house. Do you mind checking on him, please?"

"Of course," I said.

I called Maurice again. Still no answer.

"Come on, Peggy. Let's go see Maurice," I said as I grabbed my keys and headed for the car. When we arrived at Maurice's house I noticed that his car was not in the driveway.

"Wait here a second," I said to Peggy. "I'll be right back." She didn't say a word. I got out, hurried as fast as I could to his front door and rang the bell. No answer. I rang again. Still no answer. I returned to my car and drove back home. It was getting dark and I needed to feed Peggy and get her to bed.

Soon after we walked into the house, the phone rang.

"Hello?" I asked.

Dead silence, although I could tell somebody was on the line.

"Maurice, is that you?"

"Yes, Sam, it's me," he whispered. "I got your messages. Sorry I made you nervous. I had a few things to do."

"Maurice," I spoke steadily into the receiver. "I came by your house and you weren't there. Where are you? Is everything OK?"

Dead silence again.

"Maurice, are you still there?"

"Yes, Sam, I'm here. I appreciate your concern, but the bureaucrats don't give a damn. The insurance company doesn't either. You're my only friend, Sam. Please...."

It sounded like he hung up.

"Maurice? Maurice, you still there?"

No response. I called his house and got no answer. I began to tremble. I hurried into the kitchen to check on Peggy, who sat quietly at the table clutching a spoon. Her bowl was turned over and ice cream was on the floor. As I headed over to help her, I tripped and fell.

Peggy squawked. I lay there for a few moments wiggling everything to make sure they still worked — my hands, my fingers, my feet, my legs — then slowly I got back up.

"I'm OK, Peggy. No harm done." I grabbed a roll of paper towels from the counter and cleaned the ice cream off the floor.

"Peggy," I said, trying to calm myself. "Let me wipe your hands." I held out a clean towel, she took it and rubbed her hands together rapidly. I guided her to the sink, turned on the faucet and said, "Now wash your hands," which she did.

"We need to go back to Maurice's," I said. She remained quiet. I held out my arm, she grabbed onto me and out the door we went. I talked calmly and continuously to Peggy all the way to Maurice's house. Peggy hummed, babbled and looked out the window.

My stomach was in knots as if someone had punched me in the gut. Time slowed down. I pulled into the driveway, killed the engine, got out and walked as quickly as I could around to the passenger side. I opened the door and took Peggy's hand. She squawked, so I grabbed a rubber ball from under the car seat, showed it to her and slipped it into my jacket pocket. Rubber balls fascinate her. I had brought the ball from the shop for her, placed it under the seat and forgotten about it.

Peggy quieted down and got out of the car. She bobbed and I shuffled to Maurice's front door. "Just call us the Odd Couple," I whispered to her as I rang the bell.

No answer. So I knocked on the door repeatedly. I grabbed the doorknob and turned. It was unlocked. I stood there wondering what to do next when someone inside pulled the door open with a bang.

My knees buckled but I managed not to fall down. Peggy remained silent. Maurice's son Philip stood there staring at us. He seemed confused.

"Philip," I said. "I'm Sam, your father's friend, and this is my granddaughter Peggy. May we come in?"

Philip stepped aside and we walked in. Maurice sat in his recliner, his back to us, in the middle of the living room. He was slumped over. My chest tightened and I felt weak.

"Maurice?" I whispered.

He said nothing.

"Maurice, are you …"

He lifted his head slowly, turned around, opened his eyes and looked at me but said nothing. He stared at the bulge in my coat pocket.

"What's that?" he asked.

"Uh, it's a ball, Maurice."

"I've been trying to get Philip to play ball with me ever since he was a child," Maurice said then slowly turned back around.

My entire body was shaking. I felt as if I were standing inside a freezer. I walked over and stood in front of him.

"You know why I've been acting like this, don't you?" Maurice sighed.

"I know you've been struggling. You haven't done anything, have you?" I asked. My eyes searched his and all around the room trying to take everything in at once. I was looking for a pill bottle or anything that would confirm my worst fears. I didn't want to find anything, but I had to know right away what, if anything, Maurice had done to himself or Philip.

"How could Philip go through life alone if I'm no longer here to help him?"

Tears rolled down Maurice's cheeks. I pulled the footstool over and sat down next to him but said nothing. Words simply would not come.

Maurice looked directly at me. "Sam, take the gun. I couldn't do it."

"Gun?"

"It's in my room, Sam, on the top shelf of my closet wrapped in a pillow case, way in the back. I didn't want Philip to find it. You'll need a chair to get up there."

"Maurice, I'll get rid of the gun. I'll call Jeff and ask him to stop by. He'll take it and get Peggy home. I'll stay here with you and Philip tonight. We can talk. OK? Everything is going to work out."

Maurice leaned back in his chair. "Thanks, Sam."

He looked around the room. "Where's Peggy?" he asked.

I slowly stood up and shuffled into the kitchen. Philip was in there on his knees on the floor, his hands at his sides fluttering like a bird. Peggy sat directly across from him, her feet in front of her and arms held close to her chest. They stared at each other as Peggy cooed like a mourning dove at dusk. That's when I saw the rubber ball in her hands. Then she leaned forward and rolled it to Philip, who caught it and rolled it back to her.

Peggy warbled and Philip flapped. They had become friends, but they didn't say a word.

CHAPTER TWELVE

Peggy was scheduled to leave us two days after the incident at Maurice's house but no one said much about it. Jeff continued to work most nights handling paperwork and the business end of his practice, but when he was home he was especially attentive to his oldest daughter. Carol canceled two trips to meet with legislative committees.

"They don't need me there as much as I'm needed here," she said, looking sad and not elaborating.

The day before the move, Kate tried hard to keep her dialogue going when she was with Peggy but would often stop, go into another room and cry.

Peggy seemed unaware of what was happening. She had an extreme screaming fit early in the day but settled down after Rosetta gave her a warm bath and combed her hair. I wondered if the aides at the Shuler Center would know to do that. Would they even care?

Carol compiled a list of Peggy's likes and dislikes, and what to do in emergencies. Giving Peggy a warm bath was critical. Carol had spoken often with the Shuler Center social worker assigned to Peggy. The woman was open and reassuring at first, but in time seemed distracted. She was very busy.

I asked Jeff if everything was set for the transition.

"As good as can be expected I think. But it's frustrating. I'm worried about being at the mercy of the system. Peggy won't be able to tell us if she's being ignored or mistreated. I'm thinking it will be all rules and little compassion. Know what I mean?"

"Carol Geller knows what to do," I reminded Jeff. "She can charm them, she can intimidate them and she knows as much about disabilities as anyone. And don't forget Rosetta's sister Martha works there. She'll keep a close eye on Peggy."

That's when Jeff told me about Carol's surprise visit to Shuler earlier in the week.

"She was in the residential section and the staff had the residents doing household chores to get them up and moving. That's common — they want the residents to stay active as much as possible. It builds a sense of community when they work together.

"Everyone was busy folding clean towels and placing them neatly into piles. But as each one of them presented a stack to the supervisor, he'd drop them on the floor and tell the residents to start over again. Carol was furious."

"Did they understand what was happening?" I asked.

"Some did, some didn't. Carol told the supervisor he should be ashamed of himself; that he was cynical and cruel. She reminded him that each resident was human and deserved respect."

Carol complained to Shuler's administrator, who promised to look into the matter. She had not heard from the administrator since.

While Jeff and I discussed his concerns, Carol gathered Peggy's personal items, then arranged and rearranged them in her suitcase. Peggy walked in, saw the suitcase, removed everything and placed them carefully on her bed. Carol returned soon afterward and repacked Peggy's bag.

"We're taking a trip, Peggy. I know you will like it," Carol said.

Peggy quietly stared out the window.

Carol cried that afternoon as she prepared spaghetti and meatballs, Peggy's favorite meal. I wasn't sure exactly what to say.

"Are you OK with this, Carol? I mean it isn't too late to change our minds is it?" I asked.

"It really is the right thing to do, Pop. It is the right thing to do," Carol said as if she were trying to convince herself as well as me.

That night we set the table with a red-and-white checked tablecloth. In addition to pasta, Carol had prepared a tossed salad and garlic bread. I eyed the cheesecake on the counter and everyone tried to be cheerful.

"Boy, this is good spaghetti isn't it, Peggy?" Kate rambled. "And when you're not eating the meatballs you can roll them around your plate, not on the table — don't put them on the table — and look, they're like race cars. I'll bet my meatball's faster than yours. What do you think?"

Peggy lifted her spoon, pushed a meatball across her plate and onto the placemat. She looked as if she knew she'd broken a rule. Then she picked up the meatball and ate it, nodding her head vigorously. Carol put her hand on Kate's arm and reminded her that they were in the dining room, not at the Darlington Speedway. Before we left the table, Carol said breakfast would be at 7:30 because she and Peggy were going on a trip.

"Aren't we, Peggy?" Carol asked. Peggy continued bobbing her head.

Jeff said his first appointment was at 8:30 a.m. Carol glared.

"But I can be a little late," Jeff said.

The next morning, the entire household was bustling early. When I entered the kitchen, Jeff and the girls were seated at the table and Carol was serving pancakes.

"Blueberries or plain, Pop?" she asked. "It's Sandy's recipe."

"I would never turn down blueberry pancakes," I said.

"These are really good, Mom," Kate said, "but Grandma's were the best. Every time I have pancakes I think of her." Kate looked at me.

"I do too, honey," I said.

Peggy smacked her lips as she ate, trying to capture every drop of syrup that ringed her mouth and coated her fingers. The large plastic placemat in front of her was covered with bits of pancakes and blueberries, and spatters of syrup and butter. She glanced around and realized that we were looking at her.

What would happen to Peggy if she ate like this at the center? Would she be punished? What would she think? How would we ever know?

Every aggravation we had ever had with Peggy — all the inconveniences and frustrations — was insignificant now.

"It's time to go," Carol said.

Kate and I watched as Carol and Jeff walked Peggy to the car. Carol held Peggy's hand and Peggy grabbed Jeff's shirt with her other hand, legs splayed out to the sides, waddling penguin-like. When they reached the passenger side, Peggy got in and sat down. Jeff placed her suitcase in the back seat. Then he fastened her seatbelt and she screamed. Carol started the car, Kate and I waved and Jeff stepped away from the window, fluttering his hand quickly a couple of feet from Peggy's eyes.

"We love you, Peggy," Kate shouted.

"Bye, Peggy," I whispered.

But nothing happened. Carol stared out over the hood for a few moments and turned off the engine. Peggy looked up as her mother got out, walked around to the passenger side, opened the door and whispered, "No way." She turned to Jeff. "I can't do this," Carol said and began to cry.

Kate ran to the car.

Jeffrey reached out to hold Carol. "Are you sure?"

"I'm sure," she said.

Kate helped Peggy out of the car as I stood on the porch watching. I locked eyes with Peggy and smiled. Her eyes twinkled.

CHAPTER THIRTEEN

I called Irene and told her what had happened. Carol overheard me and asked that she join us for supper that night. Irene agreed. I looked forward to Jeff, Carol and the girls getting to know her. That afternoon I drove to Irene's house to pick her up and we returned just before dark.

"Ah," said Jeff upon our arrival. "So this is the woman who's stolen my Pop's heart!"

Irene smiled and her warmth filled the room. I introduced her to Peggy, who shrieked when Irene held out her hand. Irene turned her head slightly so she wasn't looking directly at Peggy and said softly, "It's nice to meet you, Peggy. Your grandfather has told me wonderful things about you."

Peggy seemed to relax and remained quiet.

We had a delightful supper. Everyone liked Irene, and she and I held hands as we were leaving.

"We hope you'll join us again soon, Irene," Carol, the world's best diplomat, said.

"Thank you, Carol," said Irene, the world's second-best diplomat. "I look forward to that."

I sighed with relief as we reached my car.

"Well, that wasn't as bad as I thought it might be," I said. "You certainly were a hit with my family."

"I'm glad to finally spend some time with them," she said as she leaned over and paused, waiting for me to kiss her. I felt a flush of embarrassment. I didn't keep her waiting even though we were still in my son's driveway.

Could that one kiss have been the reason I had unusual difficulty falling asleep that night? The whole house was quiet. Everyone had gone to bed and I was enjoying the sound of rain falling on the roof. Soon I heard thunder in the distance and I got up, which wasn't easy. I shuffled over to the window. Lighting slashed the sky, and I began to worry, which evolved into an overwhelming, irrational sensation of fear.

I got up and walked to Peggy's room. By the glow of her night-light I saw her sitting up in bed with a strange look in her eyes, far different from her usual gaze. Apparently, she was fearful too.

"Don't worry, Peggy," I said from the doorway. "It's OK."

That's when it dawned on me. Peggy understood what was going on around her to some extent. She just couldn't respond coherently.

I went to the side of her bed and sat down. "It's just thunder and lightning far away. We're safe here," I said.

She looked directly at me. My words calmed her. She lowered her head to her pillow and held her hands together as if sharing a secret handshake with herself. Soon she was sound asleep.

The rumble of thunder faded as I slipped back into my room.

• • •

Peggy and I have something special — different than anything I've ever known — a kind of telepathic anticipation. Whenever I walk into the room, she talks to me without saying a word. She relaxes and does not scream. I relax, too. I'm not self-conscious about my tremors when I'm with her. I asked Maurice one day if he and Philip experienced anything comparable.

"Heavens, no," Maurice said.

I asked Dr. Robinson if a person with Rett syndrome has an inclination to communicate in such a way with someone who has Parkinson's disease. He said he'd get back to me on that. I looked forward to my next appointment.

Parkinson's sneaks up on its victims. It will practically disappear for a while then suddenly glues your you-know-what to a chair. One out of every 10 people over the age of 70 has Parkinson's disease. It does not discriminate. Most of us don't talk about it, but it's always there. The shaking seldom stops, but folks pretend like everything is normal. They can't all be blind.

The Old Farts, of course, let nothing pass.

"For God's sake, Sam," Abe Weiss says as I quiver and deal. "You're tearing each card in two!" I always bring along a fresh deck in case I do.

Jerry Wittinger, who runs a vegetable stand just out of town, is brutally honest with me, too. He grows the freshest produce around. When tomato season starts, he's especially popular. I love to go out there and buy some. Jerry throws in some "shrink" advice for free.

"Quit prancing around like you got the jock itch," he said to me one day. "'Course, you ain't no jock. Way too nervous. At least you ain't got as far to go as you done been."

But Mr. T says I still look pretty good considering the circumstances, although he always shows me how my jaw protrudes as I slump forward.

"Meet Sam, Sam Quasimodo," he says.

But Mr. T rarely accuses me of looking depressed. When he does, I straighten up quickly and put on my game face. I tell myself I'm still the boxing champion of the world just like Muhammad Ali, not some Parkinson's chump. I will not leave the ring. Maybe it's true that the fight is rigged and the disease will win in the end.

But I'll keep swinging, and if I get to the point that I can't raise my arms, I'll keep my chin up, or out, or whatever.

• • •

It was late morning when I returned to Dr. Robinson's uncomfortable waiting room wondering if my routine three-month visit was another waste of time. I always look around that room to see if anyone is worse off than me. I've noticed that everyone else is doing the same thing. I think about getting some exercise when I'm sitting in there — like getting my rear end up off those hard chairs and sprinting back to the car.

The receptionist is red-faced, wrinkled and rotund, and never smiles. Obviously, she sleeps in a barrel of formaldehyde. Her message is always the same: "The doctor has been delayed unavoidably, but should be back in the office soon." She says this every 30 minutes on the dot. Eventually, she calls out what she thinks is my name. But it isn't "Mr. Jeller."

"Close enough," I always say. At that point, I'm in no mood to argue.

A nurse suddenly appears in the corner door and directs me to a small, windowless, cold examining room in the back where I shiver for what seems like forever again. When Dr. Robinson finally arrives, he seldom apologizes for being late.

"And how are we holding up today?" he always asks.

I'm always tempted to respond with, "You're holding me up, sir, so let's get on with it." Or, "If you're so smart, why are you asking?" Or, "Are you blind or something?" But, sadly, I always say, "I can't complain, considering the alternative. How are you, Dr. Robinson?"

He complains about how difficult it is for doctors to practice medicine nowadays, that the insurance industry is robbing him blind, that the paperwork never ends, and so on and so forth.

But this time, Dr. Robinson was not late. He walked in, looked at his chart and then at me and asked, "How are we holding up, Sam?"

"I'm getting worse."

Then he looked at me and replied: "Well, let's see why," then poked and prodded and asked me to hold up my arms. He tapped my knees with a rubber hammer and said, "You're beginning the crossover."

"The what?"

"The crossover. The disease is starting to affect both sides of your body."

"Ah," I said. "Used to be most of my problems were on my right side. Now it's on the left, too, I guess."

"The disease is progressive, but as I told you the first time you came in here, Parkinson's is not a death sentence. It's a condition that requires continuous modifications in your lifestyle."

I'd heard all this before.

"You have more symptoms since you've been diagnosed. But we're working every day on new medicines, and never forget, you're not alone with this," he said as he wrote out three new prescriptions.

I thought about Rudy Shellman handing me a shopping cart full of bags of pills.

"I'll keep you up to date with the very latest in treatments," Dr. Robinson said, "and as options arise, I'll give you as much information as I can so that you can make intelligent and informed decisions. But you have to do your part — which includes maintaining a positive attitude. Remember, if you give up, you lose."

"And if I don't, I'll win?"

"If you don't give up, you'll come back to see me again. It's your call."

Then I said, "You know, I have a granddaughter...."

"Yes, I know you do," he said. "She has Rett syndrome, and I've been thinking a lot about what you said about your special relationship with Peggy the last time you were in; that since you've been diagnosed with Parkinson's, a kind of telepathy has developed between the two of you."

I was shocked that he remembered.

Then Dr. Robinson looked straight into my eyes and said: "Love speaks."

"Love speaks?"

"Yeah, Sam. Even though she can't express herself in words, she can talk. Your grandchild understands you and you understand her. When she hurts, you hurt. It's about empathy. It's something I never learned in medical school, but I see it all the time here in this office, in the waiting room. My patients with Alzheimer's and dementia, my stroke patients, my Parkinson's patients — many of them can't speak at all. They sit quietly with their families. But if you listen carefully, you can hear them talking to each other across the room. It's in their eyes, Sam, it's in their eyes."

CHAPTER FOURTEEN

I've thought a lot about what Dr. Robinson said about love, and it occurred to me that I've not fully expressed it with my son. As I said earlier, I've never taken the time to really get to know Jeffrey. We seldom have the kind of conversations a parent and child are supposed to have. We've never fully understood each other.

And ever since Abe Weiss suggested that Jeff and Carol are having marital problems, I wasn't able to say with authority that Abe was full of crap. So I decided to do something very unusual — ask Jeff about it face to face.

Early one Saturday morning I called my son from the shop and invited him to join me for lunch again in the park. "We can get together before you go play golf," I said.

"Well, Pop, thanks for asking, but Carol and Kate have gone shopping and Rosetta won't be here until this afternoon. I'm sitting with Peggy right now."

"Bring her along," I said. "She'll enjoy getting out."

"Bring Peggy to lunch? Are you serious?"

"Why not? We'll go to the park's play area. It's fenced, and there's plenty to keep her occupied there."

"Can't we just talk about whatever is on your mind tonight

over supper?"

"No, Jeff. We can't. I'll order for all three of us and meet you there at noon."

"Well, alright," Jeff said. "I'll bring ear plugs in case she starts screaming and try to read your lips."

David from the deli delivered a large bag of lunches. "You having a party, Pop?" he asked. "This is way more food than usual."

"I'm meeting my son and granddaughter in the park."

"Sounds like fun," he said.

"Fun? Well, maybe," I said as we both left the shop. I was sitting on a bench in the play area when Jeff and Peggy arrived. He walked in front and she followed.

"See Peggy, there's Pop," Jeff said, careful not to look directly at his daughter, fearful she might scream. "Pop's got lunch for us."

Peggy walked to me, plopped down into the sandbox, and tumbled over and shrieked, drawing stares from everybody in the park. She sat up, dug her hands into the warm sand and threw it over her head. A bright grin spread across her face as she dipped her hands into the sand again.

Unsure of what Peggy wanted to eat, I had ordered her a banana, fudge stick, muffin, small carton of ice cream, container of lasagna and cup of iced lemonade. Jeff found his turkey sandwich and Diet Coke in the bag then handed me my chopped liver on rye.

"Don't you ever get tired of this?" he asked.

"Haven't yet," I shrugged.

Peggy went straight for the ice cream. Jeff pulled off the lid and she stuck her tongue in and began licking.

"Here's a spoon, Peggy," he said, but she paid no attention and grabbed a fistful of ice cream. I took out a napkin in a failed attempt to wipe off her face and hands. That's when I noticed that Jeff was staring at an attractive young woman who was pushing a red-haired boy on the swing set. She waved to him and smiled.

"Jeff, did I ever tell you about the time Pat was having an affair with a woman who used to come by the shop?" I asked.

"Pat Taylor? Are you kidding? He's an old man!" Jeffrey said.

"Yes, Pat. It happened 20 years ago, and I didn't realize what was going on until the rumors started." I looked directly at Jeff and added, "People do talk about such things you know. It's human nature."

"Geez. I just can't picture Pat having an affair...."

"It shouldn't be that hard to imagine. Temptations abound," I said then nodded toward the swing set. "Even in a playground."

Jeffrey put down his sandwich and glared at me. "What are you getting at?"

I thought about my father, who practically spoke to me from the grave: "Quiet, Samuel, aren't there enough things to worry about in this world? Keep your mouth shut and your eyes half-closed. You'll be a lot happier, and so will everyone else."

"Jeffrey," I said. "I've always respected your privacy. I should have been more active in your life, but the fact that I wasn't did not mean I didn't care. I didn't know how."

Jeff looked surprised. "You're a great father, Pop. You did the best you could."

Ouch! 'You did the best you could'?

"I kind of hoped that you'd come to me and ask important questions, Jeff. You know, I wanted you to want to talk like father to son."

"Well," Jeff said, "you seemed like you didn't want to be bothered, as if you were too busy."

"I'm sorry about that Jeff. I didn't mean to be distant. There were far more important things to do than balance my books and mow the lawn and...."

"You kept a good-looking yard," Jeff said. "I pay a crew to do mine."

"All those things seemed important to me back then," I said.

"It's not easy being a father," Jeffrey said as he looked over at the blonde woman and her red-haired son. "Life isn't easy for any of us."

His brow creased and his shoulders slumped.

"You see that woman in the blue shorts?" Jeff asked.

"Yes, I do."

"That's Wendy Spencer. She's been seeing my partner, Allen; has been for almost a year."

"Allen?" I asked. "Isn't he married?"

"Yes. He and Leah have three children. He told me about it a few months ago. Allen doesn't know what to do."

"It's a small town," I said.

"He's devoted to his kids, and worries he'll lose touch with them if he and Leah split up."

"Even when a divorce is friendly, or as much so as it can be, that's always a possibility," I said. "Frankly, I've never understood why someone with the responsibilities of a wife and children would invest in an affair."

"Invest?" Jeffrey asked. "This isn't the stock market."

"No, but I'm a businessman. Is it worth it?"

"Well, I'm not a businessman," Jeff said. "I do a lot of paperwork but my office manager and accountant handle the money. When things get complicated, I try to keep it simple. Having an affair is not simple. Having an affair is lying, and telling lies is not easy."

I looked down at Peggy playing in the sand then over at the lake where a gaggle of geese gathered along the shore.

Are geese monogamous?

Jeff continued, "Wendy Spencer is a good person. She taught school until her son came along. But Allen is a jerk. He makes a lot of money, drinks too much and allows his ego to run his life.

That's more important to him than his wife and children. He's a very unhappy man. I've spent a lot of time with him lately, mostly on the golf course, trying to talk through all this stuff with him."

"I've noticed that you have been out of the office a lot," I said. "But I didn't know why. I thought you were trying to get some exercise and improve your game."

Jeff stood up, put his hands together as if he were clutching a golf club and moved them back and forth.

"My game's terrible, Pop."

He looked at me again.

It suddenly dawned on me. "You're counseling him?"

"I wouldn't call it counseling. I'm not that kind of a doctor. I play golf with him and we talk while we're out there. I tell him how much it means to me to have an honest, loving relationship with my wife, that I wouldn't know what I'd do without Carol and the girls."

He paused, reflected a bit and continued. "Kate will be going to college soon and I want to spend as much time with her as I can before that happens. But she's so busy. It's really hard. And Peggy is a miracle. She accomplishes so much with so little. Whenever I have a big problem I think of her. Then I ask myself, 'What are you complaining about? Taxes? A sore shoulder from too much golf? A car that won't start? Are you kidding?'"

Tears welled up in the corners of my eyes. "I know exactly what you mean, son. But I've never heard you talk about it."

"Well, you know how it is, Pop. People have trouble talking about things that really matter. It's easy to talk about the Yankees...."

"First place," I pointed out. "Though their weak bullpen scares me."

"Right," Jeff laughed. "But you know what I mean."

We both looked at Peggy. She grabbed the half-sandwich that I hadn't eaten and finished it off. Jeff laughed. "She likes chopped liver! Who knew?"

"Why wouldn't she?" I asked. "She's got her grandfather's genes."

Suddenly Peggy lurched forward, her mouth opening and closing, but no sounds came out. Her face turned bright red.

"Peggy?" I asked. "Are you all right?"

Before I could move, Jeff was on his knees behind Peggy and wrapped his arms around her body below her ribcage. She gagged as she looked at me, terrified. Jeff locked his hands together and squeezed hard. Her upper body jerked forward. Then Jeff did it again and again until food dislodged from her throat.

Peggy gasped desperately for breath. People at the playground moved away, all but Wendy Spencer. She ran over to us and asked if we needed help.

"We're fine, Wendy," Jeff said. "Thanks."

"My God, Jeff," I said, loud enough so he could hear me over Peggy. "You saved her life."

"I had help from 'upstairs'," Jeff said.

Wendy walked back to the swings and her son.

Tears streaked Peggy's face as Jeff and I helped her to her feet. Her eyes were clamped shut and she screamed all the way to Jeff's car.

CHAPTER FIFTEEN

I can't describe how thrilling it is that Peggy and I take walks together. Our outings are unlike any other. For Peggy to respond immediately to a request to put on her coat because we are "going outside for a walk" took years of effort.

"Are you two going on your long stroll around the park or the short one around the block?" Carol asked, as she reached for Peggy's coat and hat the other day.

"Don't wait up for us," I smiled.

Peggy and I are an incredibly odd couple. People stop and stare as we pass — I shuffle along like an old tortoise while Peggy wobbles like a penguin 10 paces behind. If I slow down to close ranks, her personal-space defense system goes off and she screams. Both of us must be careful with every step. One of us could easily trip and fall.

Once as we crossed the street, Peggy sat down halfway across, *in the middle of the road* and refused to move. I managed to get the cars to stop and convinced her we should move. She has no sense of impending danger. Peggy allows me to hold her hand occasionally and sometimes she takes me by my arm. She seems to know how important this is to me. I feel her love and I think she feels mine. It's a wonderful thing to walk with her — a wonderful thing to be able to walk at all.

I realize that neither of us may be able to walk one day. But I try to stay positive. I live one step at a time. The rewards are great when you understand that life is a blessing.

• • •

I was surprised recently when Peggy handed me a special gift. Immediately after she placed it in my hand, she turned abruptly and held her hands over her face.

My gift was a small, flat piece of wood with a circle painted in the center. I had seen her hunched over a block of wood working intensely with Rosetta's help. Peggy used sandpaper to smooth its corners and a purple marker to make the distinctive ring in the center. It's a symbol of her love.

She always makes sure I have her gift nearby. I woke up this morning and it was on the pillow beside me. She came into my room while I slept and placed it there. My wooden sculpture with the purple circle is more precious than gold.

The other day, we went for our walk and the weather was lovely and the air crisp, so we headed to the park. We passed a group of college students, laughing and enjoying their youth. Peggy and I were enjoying our lives, too, although we weren't young anymore. I saw the ice cream parlor across from the bank and decided to stop in for a cone. I was careful, making sure I didn't trip and she didn't wander out into the traffic. My medications were working and I was not sleepy. I felt no serious tremors and my legs seemed strong.

As we entered the ice cream shop, I turned to guide Peggy toward the soda fountain and down I went. People with Parkinson's often have a distorted sense of balance. I remember being on the floor and trying to move my hands and feet. I tried to sit up and got very dizzy. Everything spun, so I laid back and listened to the jumble of voices all around me.

"Where's my granddaughter?" I asked, but no one was listening. All I heard was: "Lie still, mister. Does anything hurt? Can you feel your arms?"

"Where's Peggy?" I kept asking. "You don't understand. I need to know where she is."

"Call an ambulance! Call EMS!" somebody yelled.

As they lifted me into the ambulance I pleaded for help finding Peggy. "I'm here with my granddaughter! I can't leave without her!"

Carol insists that we make sure Peggy is wearing her ID bracelet whenever we leave the house. But I forgot that day. I remember hearing the siren before I passed out. I awoke inside the emergency room to a female nurse calling for a brain scan.

"Peggy!" I asked. "Where is Peggy?"

"Be quiet. You're in the hospital," the nurse said as she strapped me down and gently adjusted the oxygen mask over my nose. I was helpless.

"Stay calm, you'll be fine," the head nurse kept saying.

"Do I have a choice?" I asked.

"Find Peggy" were my last words before drifting out of consciousness.

• • •

"Good morning, Mr. Geller. How are you feeling?" asked the neurosurgery resident still in his green scrub suit. His cheerful manner belied the fact that he had no sleep all night.

I opened my eyes and was blinded by the light. My head pounded like a jackhammer.

"My granddaughter, Peggy," I said. "Have you found her?"

"She's fine, and you are too. You had a subdural hematoma, which means you were bleeding inside your skull. We relieved the pressure and you're doing very well."

"Where's Peggy?" I asked.

"She's safe at home. Your family can tell you the whole story. Your son has been here with you most of the night. He'll be back soon."

Relieved, I closed my eyes and dozed off until Jeff, Carol and Kate arrived. Kate held a bouquet of flowers.

"Is Peggy OK?" I asked.

"She had quite an adventure," Jeff said. "The police found her in the parking lot of an abandoned tattoo parlor near the ice cream shop. She made some friends while the police were looking for her. She was calm and collected when the officers arrived."

"Friends?" I asked.

"The police found Peggy sitting on old blankets with four men and a woman, all of them homeless. The woman said Peggy was wandering in the traffic in front of the ice cream shop. So she led Peggy by the hand to her friends in the parking lot for safekeeping. Then the woman went back to the ice cream parlor and asked the owner to call the police. Peggy was sitting quietly with them when the police arrived."

"Quietly?" I asked. "Amazing. We've got to thank those folks."

"We will, Pop."

"You're sure Peggy's OK?"

"She's home with Rosetta right now. By the way, I called Irene and told her what happened. She said to give you her love."

"She did?" I asked, unable to suppress a little smile.

Jeff handed me my wooden sculpture, as I closed my eyes and drifted off to sleep.

CHAPTER SIXTEEN

When I woke up, my head no longer ached. I was happy that my "noggin" was as hard as Pat has been telling me it is for 20 years. I sat up in my bed thinking about this when I heard tapping at the door. In walked Irene.

"Hello, Sam," she said as she walked over and kissed me on my cheek. "The sign on the door said 'No Visitors' but I just had to see you. You look great, Sam. You're as handsome as ever."

"Have I died and gone to Heaven?" I asked.

"You're just fine, my dear," Irene whispered in my ear.

"I feel better now that you're here," I said. "Wanna play nurse?"

I hadn't seen Irene in a week, and I missed her. And if you haven't figured it out yet, we're more than just friends now. Old people do fall in love.

"Your kisses are a miracle drug," I told her.

She giggled. "Sam, you're funny and sweet and an excellent salesman, too. Whether you're peddling a second-hand banjo or seducing an old bird like me, you're the best."

I reached out for her hand and our fingers intertwined. I felt like we were teenagers on a Ferris wheel ride.

"Irene, what would become of us if I never got out of here."

"What kind of question is that?"

"Seriously, Irene, would you still want to be with me?"

"Sam, I prefer to live in the present, not the future. I'm here with you now, and that's all that matters. I was going to wait to see you after you left the hospital, but I just couldn't do it. I'm so relieved that you are in good shape and that Peggy is safe. Jeff and Carol told me about the people who helped her."

"Irene, you know how I told you that the worse my Parkinson's gets, the better I'm able to communicate with Peggy?"

Irene nodded.

"Those folks got through to Peggy, too."

CHAPTER SEVENTEEN

The religious holidays have always been important in the Geller family. Passover, which is celebrated in the spring, is my favorite. It's a wonderful family tradition, especially the first-night supper, which we call the Seder. This is when we read the story of the Exodus of the Israelites from slavery in remembrance of their dash for freedom from Egypt.

The Passover meal is a grand celebration. We recite the ancient stories, chant the songs and partake of the ritual foods, all of which link us to our ancestors.

So we gather each year with family and friends and enjoy the traditions (whether or not we believe in the actual parting of the Red Sea). The Jewish faith is welcoming and enduring.

For many years Sandy and I had the honor of conducting the Seder in our home along with our families and friends, Jews and non-Jews. Memories of past Seders remain clear to me. In my mind's eye, I see the people who shared those meals: my parents, my grandfather, my brother, Sandy's parents and siblings, and many friends.

I remember the year I knocked over a bottle of wine and soaked the table; the time my father thought he was having a heart attack and we rushed him to the emergency room to learn with great relief it was only heartburn. And there was the Passover when we forgot to buy the wine we needed for the meal. Fortunately, we had a neighbor who had a wine cellar and some surplus kosher red.

I was overjoyed when Jeff and Carol told me they were ready to accept the responsibility of hosting the Seder this year. "Are you sure you want all that work?" I asked Carol.

"It's our turn, Pop," she said as she looked around the living room. "Besides, this place could stand a good cleaning."

"I can push a vacuum," I offered.

"Don't worry about that," she said and looked over at Jeff sitting on the couch and reading the newspaper. "Everyone will pitch in."

Jeff raised the pages over his head and feigned innocence. "I can't imagine what you're talking about," he said before hiding again behind the paper.

The hosts of the Passover Seder spend weeks preparing for the meal.

Some Jews are hardcore religionists. They adhere inflexibly to tradition. They prefer the Seder to be conducted as it was in my childhood, when it lasted at least six hours. Nowadays, good luck keeping children sitting down for six hours during a family gathering with some food they don't particularly like!

This year I arose on Passover morning long before the sun did. I walked through the dimly lit hallway and into the dining room. The table was set and the silverware gleamed. The room was spotless and quiet. I had the strange sensation that at any minute someone would snap on the lights, the singing would begin and all of the excitement that I remembered from past Seders would fill the room.

My reflections were interrupted by the appearance of a sleepy-looking, pajama-clad man. Jeffrey rubbed his eyes and yawned. "Pop, what are you doing?"

"Checking everything out," I said.

"Relax, I can handle it."

"You sure?"

"I'm sure, Pop. Don't worry. And I'll open the door for Elijah. We certainly don't want to miss him."

Elijah was an ancient prophet who is honored during the Seder. The celebrants' door is left open and a special goblet of red wine is poured just for him. If you keep a close eye on that cup you'll see the wine jiggle from time to time as if someone is drinking it.

Could it be Elijah?

Elijah represents hope, freedom from oppression — physical and psychological — and a better life for all humanity.

"What are you doing up so early?" I asked Jeff.

"I'm wired, Pop. I hope our ancestors appreciate the way we continue the Passover tradition. What would Gramps say?"

"He'd be proud."

"I hope so, Pop. I'm going to try to go back to bed for a while. It's going to be a big day."

• • •

In the late afternoon, well before sundown, the guests began to arrive. The first was Saul, my best Old Fart friend. Saul's wife died less than a year ago and his kids live far away. It was a great pleasure to spend time with him away from the card table or in his office.

Maurice came, too. He hired a sitter for Philip and accepted our invitation with delight. "You're good to include me after what I've put you through," he said.

"That's what friends are for," I said.

I'm not sure what was responsible for his new attitude — a change in medications, his counselor's insights or perhaps a new balance in his view of things, but Maurice was genuinely happy.

Kate, now a freshman in college, arrived at the same time Irene did. They greeted each other as if they were life-long friends.

Pat Taylor rang the doorbell looking as disheveled as usual. He's been joining us for Seder for years.

In the past, Peggy always made a brief appearance and this time we hoped she would join us at the table. Carol set a place for Peggy at my right. She preferred to sit in her usual protective position, a few feet away out of touching range of anyone she didn't know. But setting that place for her was important.

Rosetta was invited but opted to celebrate Easter with her family. "If you need me to take care of my girl, you just say so. I'm never too busy for Peggy," she told us.

Jeffrey sat at the head of the table at my left. As he looked around at everyone, he took my hand and squeezed it: "This is the first Seder we have been honored to host in our home." He swallowed, paused, looked first at Carol, then at me. "Before we begin, I ask my father, as host of our previous family Seders, to speak."

The late afternoon sun filled the room with warmth. Time stopped for a moment before my words began to flow: "Quite frankly, I'm relieved to turn over the responsibility of leading this Seder to my son. As you all know, I have been struggling with a nasty disease. I have had a lot of help fighting it but ultimately it's a battle that is solely my own. I am pleased that my son has taken charge of this special celebration. He is a strong link in the chain that goes back many centuries to our ancestors who were led out of slavery to freedom, and thanks to them we continue to remember the Exodus."

I turned to Jeffrey and said, "Son, I am proud of you. Please proceed."

Jeff raised his wine goblet and began with a Hebrew chant: "In every generation, we must see ourselves as if we personally were liberated from Egypt...."

My hands would have trembled excessively if I held up that cup. It would have been difficult for me to see the text, to recite the words. My time has passed. Jeffrey, now in the prime of his life, has taken my place. The tradition continues, as does the circle of life.

I said a silent prayer, so thankful that I was still alive. It was a profound blessing to be among the people I love. The Yiddish word *qvell*, which means "immense pride," best described my feelings at that moment. The songs were sung with their usual vigor in celebration of God's bountiful gifts to the Jewish people. At one point I asked Jeffrey, "Do you remember the way your grandmother used to talk about all the ways of being enslaved? She used to say, 'You can be a slave to work, to destructive habits, to greed, to ego.' Well, I'm here to tell you we can be slaves to horrible diseases, too, but only if we allow it. I will not let my Parkinson's ruin my life."

I glanced across the table, smiled at Irene and her eyes twinkled. Saul looked at me with a wide grin and raised his glass in a silent toast. Pat and the others did the same.

As I was saying earlier, there is a portion of the Seder service that is especially meaningful, whimsical even. Jews believe that the coming of the Messiah will be preceded by a return of Elijah. So it's customary to open the door late in the service to welcome the great prophet.

This is a folk tradition, and it has provided some hilarious situations over the years. Rainy nights always bring forth queries on why the heck would Elijah be out on such a nasty night. There is a custom in our family that the single women of marriageable age must hold their candles high as the front door is opened, raising them to the height of the man they hope to marry.

When Kate was in grade school and enamored with basketball star Michael Jordan, she stood on a stool to raise her candle high enough. The belief is that as Elijah comes in the door he will make note of these requests and fulfill them. Also, his special glass of wine is placed at the center of the Seder table to keep him happy.

Kate, who was the youngest in the room this year, took up her candle and said, "We could use some more children here if you don't mind."

Peggy had not joined us at the table yet. She sat quietly on the floor near the kitchen door and her eyes were aglow. Carol had given her a small flashlight rather than a candle. As we were all looking around for Elijah, a bright cone of light illuminated the dining room chandelier and the wine glasses sparkled.

"What the …?" I blurted out.

I looked over at Peggy. She had clicked on the flashlight and aimed it above our heads, providing the evening's special effects. She then placed the light on the floor, stood up, ambled over to the chair next to me, sat down and rested her head on my shoulder. I looked at Elijah's glass, and it was jiggling.

• • •

I don't know how many Seders are ahead of me. My disease keeps advancing, but, thankfully, more slowly than I feared it would. And Peggy keeps baffling the doctors who didn't think she would reach her 10th birthday.

I wonder, is it a miracle of Elijah that gives us wisdom, strength and health to transform curses into blessings — so much so that even while suffering the ravages of horrible diseases we find it a blessing to care for others who desperately need help? People have pitied Peggy and tried to console Carol and Jeff for having a child like her. Some wonder how they have managed to keep Peggy in their home and not in an institution. Few realize the exceptional joy she brings to us, and how much we have learned about love from her.

It's taken 80 years and a debilitating disease for me to fully understand and appreciate the gift of love. It's taken all that time and all the experiences of my life to understand how important it is to communicate with one another. And what I'm finding is not a wilderness that I must wander alone, but an amazing path on which I do not have to watch my step for fear of falling.

ABOUT THE AUTHOR

Dr. Charles H. Banov was born in Charleston, South Carolina into a family of natural storytellers in the days before television and social media. He is a graduate of Emory University and the Medical College of South Carolina in Charleston where he received his M.D. in 1955. Following training at Milwaukee County Hospital, he spent two years as a Navy medical officer in Texas. He took further training in internal medicine at Charity Hospital in New Orleans, followed by a fellowship at Massachusetts General Hospital (Harvard Medical School). He was a Clinical Professor of Medicine at the Medical University of South Carolina and was elected to AOA, the honorary medical organization. He practiced allergy and immunology in Charleston from 1961 until his retirement in 2007.

Dr. Banov was a founding member of the South Carolina Society for Autistic Children in 1971 and was the first president of this organization. He was also president of numerous state and local organizations during his time as an active civic leader.

He served as president of the American College of Allergy and the world organization of asthma, Interasma. As a teacher and professor he taught at MUSC and has lectured extensively worldwide.

He has volunteered as a reserve medical officer in the Israel Defense Forces (IDF) and during Hurricane Hugo in South Carolina. He also provided medical aid in Texas after Hurricane Katrina.

After retiring, Dr. Banov penned his memoir, "Office Upstairs, a Doctor's Journey." "Love Is Two People Talking" is his first novel.

Dr. Banov is married to Nancy, his wife of 55 years, and they have 4 children and 6 grandchildren.

Resources for Parkinson's Disease

American Parkinson Disease Association
135 Parkinson Ave
Staten Island, NY 10305-1425
apda@apdaparkinson.org
http://www.apdaparkinson.org
Phone: 718-981-8001
Fax: 718-981-4399

Parkinson Alliance
P.O. Box 308
Kingston, NJ 08528-0308
admin@parkinsonalliance.org
http://www.parkinsonalliance.org
Phone: 609-688-0870
Fax: 609-688-0875

Parkinson's Action Network (PAN)
1025 Vermont Avenue, NW
Suite 1120
Washington, D.C. 20005
info@parkinsonsaction.org
http://www.parkinsonsaction.org
Phone: 800-850-4726
Fax: 202-638-7257

The Parkinson's Institute and Clinical Center
675 Almanor Avenue
Sunnyvale, CA 94085
info@thepi.org
http://www.thepi.org
Phone: 408-734-2800
Fax: 408-734-8522

WE MOVE (Worldwide Education and Awareness for Movement Disorders)
5731 Mosholu Avenue
Bronx, NY 10024
wemove@wemove.org
http://www.wemove.org
Phone: 347-843-6132
Fax: 718-601-5112

Davis Phinney Foundation
4676 Broadway
Boulder, CO 80304
info@davisphinneyfoundation.org
http://www.davisphinneyfoundation.org
Phone: 866-358-0285
Fax: 303-733-3350

National Parkinson Foundation
1501 N.W. 9th Avenue
Bob Hope Road
Miami, FL 33136-1494
contact@parkinson.org
http://www.parkinson.org
Phone: 305-243-6666
Fax: 305-243-5595

Michael J. Fox Foundation for Parkinson's Research
Church Street Station
P.O. Box 780
New York, NY 10008-0780
http://michaeljfox.org
Phone: 212-509-0995

Parkinson's Disease Foundation (PDF)
1359 Broadway
Suite 1509
New York, NY 10018
info@pdf.org
http://www.pdf.org
Phone: 212-923-4700
Fax: 212-923-4778

Parkinson's Resource Organization
74-478 Highway 111
No 102
Palm Desert, CA 92260
info@parkinsonsresource.org
http://www.parkinsonsresource.org
Phone: 760-773-5628
Fax: 760-773-9803

Bachmann-Strauss Dystonia & Parkinson Foundation
Fred French Building 551 Fifth Avenue, at 45th Street
Suite 520
New York, NY 10176
info@bsdpf.org
http://www.dystonia-parkinsons.org
Phone: 212-682-9900
Fax: 212-987-0662

Resources for Rett Syndrome

BRAIN
P.O. Box 5801
Bethesda, MD 20824
Phone: 800-352-9424
http://www.ninds.nih.gov

International Rett Syndrome Foundation
4600 Devitt Drive
Cincinnati, OH 45246
admin@rettsyndrome.org
http://www.rettsyndrome.org
Phone: 513-874-3020

National Institute of Child Health and Human Development (NICHD) National Institutes of Health, DHHS
31 Center Drive, Rm. 2A32 MSC 2425
Bethesda, MD 20892-2425
http://www.nichd.nih.gov
Phone: 301-496-5133
Fax: 301-496-7101

Office of Rare Diseases
National Institutes of Health, DHHS
6100 Executive Blvd., 3B01, MSC 7518
Bethesda, MD 20892-7518
http://rarediseases.info.nih.gov
Phone: 301-402-4336

Easter Seals
233 South Wacker Drive
Suite 2400
Chicago, IL 60606
info@easterseals.com
http://www.easterseals.com
Phone: 312-726-6200
Fax: 312-726-1494

National Institute of Mental Health (NIMH)
National Institutes of Health, DHHS
6001 Executive Blvd. Rm. 8184, MSC 9663
Bethesda, MD 20892-9663
nimhinfo@nih.gov
http://www.nimh.nih.gov
Phone: 301-443-4513
Fax: 301-443-4279

Rett Syndrome Research Trust
67 Under Cliff Road
Trumbull, CT 06611
monica@rsrt.org
http://www.rsrt.org
Phone: 203-445-0041